Hand-Turned Tales

Jude Knight

Published by Jude Knight at CreateSpace
Copyright 2016 Judith Anne Knighton writing as Jude Knight

ISBN 978-0-473-34176-3

Cover image: Penning a Letter, by George Goodwin Kilburne

Dedication

To my readers, who inspire me to try harder and do better.

Come sample my tales

The stories in this book were written as 'Made-to-Order' competition prizes. The winner chose three characters or objects and a story trope. What I did after that was up to me; the raw material of these ideas turned on the lathe of my imagination.

And so you are about to read three short stories and a novella. I offer them as a sample of my writing style, the stories I love to tell, and the types of hero and heroine I love creating. I hope you enjoy following my characters through the turns in their tales.

Thank you to Crystal Cox, Tiffany Reid, Mary Anne Landers, and Carol Cork, who planted the seeds that became these stories.

Table of Contents

The Raven's Lady

Felix returns home in disguise after thirteen years away from home. He plans to catch a smuggler, then take up his viscountcy. He does not expect the smuggler to be Joselyn, his childhood sweetheart. (Short story)

In the past eight years, Felix Maddox had spent more hours staking out suspects than he ever wished to remember. He couldn't count the number of nights he'd spent awake, knowing he'd go into battle the next morning. He had even been imprisoned for six months.

This evening, as a guest in what should be his own home, was probably not the most interminable he had ever suffered through. At this moment, though, it certainly felt like it.

The lady he was supposedly here to consider as a wife was pretty enough, he supposed, if one liked milk-and-water misses who never looked up from their plates, and who answered every conversational sally with a monosyllable or a giggle.

She had, sadly, changed from the lively child he remembered. But that was long ago, almost another life. She had been nine, and he fourteen, the last time they parted.

The only interesting thing about her now, as far as he could see, was the raven she kept as a pet. He remembered the raven, too. He'd been the one to rescue the half-fledged bird from a cat, but Joselyn Bellingham had tended it, fed it, and captured its affection.

He'd been startled earlier in the day when the raven flew in the library window, fixed him with a knowing eye, then marched out the door and along the hall, to tap at the door of Miss Bellingham's sitting room until she opened and let it in.

Now though, at dinner, any sign of originality was absent. And as for his cousin, the fat oaf who had inherited the viscountcy when Felix was reported dead, the man's conversation was all *on-dits* about people Felix didn't know and off-colour jokes that were inappropriate in front of a lady, to say nothing of not being funny.

Miss Bellingham rose to leave the gentlemen to their port, and Felix forced his face into a pleasant smile, preparing to get fat Cyril even drunker and pump him for any knowledge he had of the Black Fox, the smuggler Felix had been sent to investigate.

A waste of time, in his opinion. Cyril could not organise a bunfight in a baker's shop. The condition of the lands and buildings on the estates of Maddox Grange showed the man was a total incompetent.

Felix couldn't blame Cyril for thinking he was the viscount. Felix had decided to remain dead, to more easily find the traitors who had given him up to the French. The released prisoner, Frederick Matthews, was no threat to them, until all of the sudden, they were behind bars. Then, Colonel Webster, one of Castlereagh's men, had approached him and said the identity he had painstakingly created could be used to help England win the war.

He'd stayed in that identity even after Napoleon was exiled to Elba, sure the emperor would not accept his defeat. The right decision, as it turned out, but Waterloo had finished Napoleon's ambitions forever, and Felix was now home to reclaim his own. Just this one last job before he retired from the shadowy world he had inhabited with Webster and his ilk.

Felix had nothing against smugglers, who simply sought to make a living, but he hated, with a passion, the type Webster was after: those who had smuggled French spies onto English soil. And the Black Fox—the smuggler leader on the patch of coast that belonged to Maddox Grange—was, by all accounts, the worst of the worst.

"So what did you think of her? Nice tits, eh?" Cyril made cupping movements under his own, not inconsiderable, dugs.

Felix resisted the urge to punch the fool. "She is very quiet," he said.

"Yes, that's an advantage, don't you think," Cyril agreed. "Who wants a chattering woman? And she's a good housekeeper, don't you know? And used to living in the country, so you could just leave her at your estate. You did say you had an estate, Matthews?"

"Yes, I have an estate."

After the meeting with Webster, he'd been sitting at his club considering his options when Cyril Maddox came in with a group of cronies. That wasn't so surprising. The Maddoxes had been members of Brooks's since it opened. He hadn't recognised Cyril; he hadn't seen him since they were boys. But the group sat right behind him, and he'd soon realised that the supposed viscount was talking about raising money by selling Felix's childhood friend.

"Does Miss Bellingham have a fortune, Maddox?" one of the others asked. "I'm not interested in a chit without a fortune."

"A competence, rather. In trust till she turns twenty-five or marries," Cyril said. "If she had a fortune, Peckridge, I'd be marrying her myself! But two thousand pounds, gents! That's worth an investment of five hundred, surely? And she'll have control of it herself in less than three years. A sin against nature, that is."

"Twenty-two? That's pretty old! What's wrong with her? Second-hand, is she?" The others all sniggered.

Cyril was indignant, more on behalf of his sale than in defence of Miss Bellingham. Felix was indignant enough on that cause for both of them. He remembered Joselyn Bellingham, remembered her well. She was Cyril's cousin, not his, the daughter of Cyril's mother's sister, left to her aunt's care after the death of her parents, "and as shy and modest a lady as you could wish to find," Cyril proclaimed.

Even if he hadn't had his mission, Felix might have spoken up at that point, for the sake of the child he remembered. As it was, he introduced himself (as Frederick Matthews), apologised for overhearing, and announced that he was interested in two thousand pounds and would be willing to consider taking a wife. It worked, and here he was, drinking his own port, in his own house, and listening to Cousin Cyril describing a lady in terms that made him see red.

Suddenly, he could stand it no longer. His investigation into the Black Fox would have to wait for tomorrow. "I'm tired, Maddox," he said. "I think I'll turn in."

When Felix got to the room assigned to him—one of the guest rooms on the west frontage of the house—he couldn't sleep. Perhaps a stroll in the woods: scene of many a childhood game when he and his widowed mother had lived here with his grandfather. And a slightly older Felix often stole out on a night such as this, when the moon was nearly full, to trap game in the woods, or just to watch animals living their secret lives while the world slept.

No sooner thought than done, he let himself down from the window and was soon slipping into the shadows under the trees. As he had so many times before, he chose a trunk to lean against, stilled his movements, and slowed his breathing to wait for what the night had to show him.

There was a fox, trotting purposefully along the path. An owl swept by on silent wings. Two deer stepped daintily out of the undergrowth, then startled as they caught the fox's scent and leapt backward again, crashing away into the deeper shadows.

No. Not the fox. Someone was coming from the house. Without moving a muscle, he prepared for action. A figure, but not large enough to be Cyril. The hope that he could clear this whole matter up this first night had died, but his curiosity remained. Where was the lad going? For the person hurrying along the path was no more than a boy, surely; short and slender, with a youthful gait.

On impulse, Felix followed, using all his woodcraft to stay silent and undetected, but still keep within sight of the boy.

They took the fork leading down to the cliffs. Below, on the beach, easily visible in the moonlight, people milled around several rowboats in the surf. He'd found the smugglers after all! No legitimate cargo would be unloaded on a remote beach in the middle of the night.

The boy turned onto the path down the cliff face, but Felix would be seen if he tagged along. He concealed himself in a rocky outcrop, where he could watch both the beach and the path from the village. If the smugglers planned to take the cargo inland tonight, that was the most likely direction for whatever transport they had arranged.

As time wore on, however, it became clear the cargo was being stored in the old cave complex Felix used to explore as a child, before his mother married again and took him away. Good. He could bring a troop to watch until the smugglers came to retrieve the goods, and catch them all.

Oddly, the boy Felix had followed seemed to be directing the whole enterprise, people came to him, as if for orders, and several times, Felix saw him run into the surf to catch and redirect someone.

The rowing boats went back for another load, and another. The night was beginning to lighten in the east before the last of them had its cargo removed, and disappeared back into the waves.

Below, the smugglers began to slip away, singly and in small groups.

Something odd struck Felix, about the faces that looked up at the cliff before beginning to climb the path. No beards or moustaches. Not even the shadows one might expect after a day's growth. His mind took a while to interpret what his eyes were telling him. Women. Every smuggler he could see was a woman.

His eyes on the boy, he shook his head to dislodge the wild thought. No. Not Miss Bellingham. That milk-and-water miss could not possibly be a smuggler. The boy—or the woman, in fact—could be anyone in the house, or could easily have come from one of the farms beyond. But he was definitely a she. As the light strengthened, the way she moved, and the curves inside the breeches she wore, became more and more obvious.

Then, the raven swooped down to land on the beach beside her, and removed all doubt. Miss Bellingham's pet cawed at her, a loud raven alarm call, and she looked anxiously up at the cliff. A few quick orders to the remaining women on the beach, and they all scattered, some heading for the path, and some for the narrow way around the cliffs that had been uncovered as the tide fell.

Now what did he do? He stiffened his shoulders. Woman she may be, but also a smuggler. He would do his duty, of course. Even though once, long ago, she had been Joselyn, the girl-child who dogged his footsteps, and whom he would have died to protect.

Miss Bellingham led a few other women up the cliff face, and stopped to speak with them a few paces from where Felix hid. The raven swooped in to join them.

"It will be enough, Matilda," she was saying. "The money we raise will pay your rent, and the other tenants', and keep Cousin Cyril from casting you out."

"For another quarter, miss," the woman called Matilda said, dolefully. "We canna keep doing this here smuggling, though. If'n the Black Fox catches us, or the excise, we'll all hang."

Miss Bellingham nodded, her brows drawn anxiously together. "By next quarter, perhaps I will have thought of something else."

"Master Felix had no business dying in foreign parts," Matilda declared.

"I do not suppose he did it on purpose," Miss Bellingham said. Was it just his imagination, or did her tone sound wistful?

"If'n he'd lived, tha' could have wed him," another woman suggested. Felix recognised her; she was a servant at the grange. "Tha' always said he promised to come back and wed thee."

"He was fourteen, Betsy. Even if he had lived, he would have long forgotten a few words said in haste when his mother took him away."

"Mayhap you should marry that man your cousin brought home," Betsy said.

Miss Bellingham gave an inelegant snort. "If I were inclined to marry, and I am not, I would certainly not marry any friend of Cousin Cyril."

"He's a well-enough-looking young man," Betsy insisted, "and polite, too."

"He is prepared to pay my cousin to get his hands on my trust fund. In any case, I do not think he still wishes to marry me."

"Only for that you've gone out of your way to discourage him," Betsy said.

Miss Bellingham giggled. "I just listened to everything Cyril said he liked, and did the opposite."

Why, the little minx. Certainly, Miss Milk-and-Water was unrecognisable in the laughing maiden before him. He had told Cyril he preferred women with opinions, who could think for themselves and hold an intelligent conversation. He might have added that he wanted to wed a lady who put the welfare of his tenants ahead of her own, as this delightfully grown-up Joselyn clearly did.

The women were splitting up, Miss Bellingham and Betsy taking the wood path, followed by the raven, and the other women heading along the clifftop to the village. He watched them out of sight, but stayed where he was. He had a lot to think about. Miss Bellingham was clearly not the Black Fox, even if she was a smuggler. And she was far more the Joselyn of his memories than he had believed.

The sound of shifting rocks attracted his attention.

Two men emerged from another rocky outcrop some distance down the cliff, and walked up to the junction of the two paths, talking as they came. One was Cousin Cyril, the other a dark, burly man who walked with the distinctive roll of a sailor.

"It's my cousin, I tell you," Cyril insisted. "That damnable bird follows her everywhere."

"I don't care who it is," said his companion. "She's on my patch, and I'll have her cargo, and I'll kill anyone who gets in my way, and so I will."

"Look here, Fox!" Cyril was clearly alarmed. "You can't kill my cousin. I've got a man up at the house who's willing to pay good money to marry her."

At the scent of money, the Black Fox—for it must be he—pointed like a hound. "How much is the wench worth?"

"Two thousand pound. And this Matthews is willing to stump up five hundred to have the rest free and clear."

"Two thousand, eh? That'd go a long way to sweetening your exile!" The Fox laughed. "Worth more dead than alive, I'd say."

Cyril shook his head. "She's made a will leaving the lot to her sister's children. Not that the brats need it. They're wealthy orphans; inherited a packet when their parents died. I need her alive, I tell you."

"You could marry her yourself."

Cyril shook his head. "I tried that. She won't have a bar of it. And I've no wish for a wife, anyway."

"Drug her, marry her, and then kill her before you run," the Fox advised.

For a moment, Cyril looked interested, but then he shook his head. "Too complicated. I couldn't have the banns called. Even if I had time to wait—and the real Viscount Maddox could turn up at any time—no one here would believe she was willing. I'm just lucky I heard two men discussing his unexpected survival and his petition to the courts to be recognised as viscount. It has given me a little warning to sell everything off. Once the courts notify me, I'll not be able to touch a penny."

"A special licence?"

"Expensive. And chancy—she could still refuse me at the church. No, getting this Matthews fellow to court her is the best plan."

"Or..." The Fox fell silent, clearly thinking deeply.

"Or?" Cyril prompted.

"I could buy her off you. I'll pay four hundred pound, mind, and not a penny more! But I'll be able to sell her to the Barbary pirates, a fair-haired virgin like that. She is a virgin, I suppose?"

Cyril nodded, eagerly.

"Yes," the Fox continued. "It's only fair, the trouble she's caused me, taking cargoes on my patch. Yes, and I'll take my pick of the other women she had with her." He grinned, an evil leer that made Felix shiver. "Some to sell, and some to use on the way."

"Four fifty," Cyril said, "and you have a bargain. What's the plan, then?"

The two men moved out of earshot, still talking. Felix hurried after as soon as they cleared the open ground and went into the trees, but they had horses tied in a small clearing, and he caught up only to see them ride away.

Time to return to the house, then, Felix thought. And past time for a conversation with the lady smuggler.

When Felix got back to the house, he could not find Miss Bellingham. However, he found the servant, Betsy.

"Tell Miss Bellingham, please, that I heard her cousin, Cyril, and the Black Fox plotting against her, and I need to see her now. I'll wait in the library."

After a shocked moment, Betsy hurried upstairs, and a few minutes later, Miss Bellingham entered the room.

She'd clearly been interrupted before she could complete her change of clothes. She'd put on a dress, but her hair was caught back in a long plait that brushed her rump as she walked. Betsy came in at her shoulder, and their glares were identical.

"Mr Matthews? What's this about my cousin?"

"Not Matthews," Felix told her. "My name is not Matthews. I was sent here to investigate the Black Fox for the Crown. I followed you last night, and I saw you bringing in your cargo."

Now the women had identical looks of alarm.

"It is not what you think," Miss Bellingham said. "I am not the Black Fox. And the women—they were just following my orders. I am the leader. Arrest me. Let them go."

"No, Miss," Betsy objected. "We all agreed. We're all in this."

"None of you are in this," Felix said. "I'm not after you. I want the Black Fox. In any case, Miss Bellingham, I don't wish to arrest an old friend, and I certainly don't intend to arrest the wives and daughters of my tenants."

Betsy was bewildered, but Miss Bellingham was examining him with narrowed eyes. "You are dead," she told him.

"No," he said.

She was shaking her head. "We were told you were dead."

Joselyn still got a white, pinched look around her lips when she was angry, Felix noted, and two bright spots of colour on her cheeks.

"I'm sorry," he said, not sure what he was apologising for.

"You should be. I cried. I wore black for a year. Why are you not dead, Felix?" And then she was in his arms, punching his shoulder and fighting back tears. "I am so glad you are not dead."

He tightened his arms around her, but Betsy cleared her throat, and Miss Bellingham pushed away.

"You be Viscount Maddox, seemingly?" Betsy asked. "Come to take yer own, is it?"

"After we catch the Black Fox and Cousin Cyril, yes," Felix said. He was finding it hard to focus on the job ahead of them, given how wonderfully Miss Bellingham filled his arms, and how empty they now felt without her. The idea of redeeming his boyhood promise was growing more and more appealing.

"Where have you been? Why have you waited so long to come home?" That was his Joselyn, ever pestering him with questions.

"I will answer every question you have," he told her. "But we don't have time today. Today, we have to decide what to do with your enemies."

Quickly, he told the two women what he'd overheard. Then he had to repeat it for most of the rest of the household. Not, however, the valet or the butler who, Joselyn said, were from London and were Cyril's men through and through. The local people, she said, could be trusted.

When Felix had finished his story, the servants were of a single mind.

"You can't go, then, Miss," said Betsy. "We'll have to let the Black Fox have the cargo."

"We can't risk you, Miss," one of the other servants said, and the others murmured their approval.

Joselyn turned to Felix. "I suppose they are right. But I hate letting Cyril and the Black Fox win."

"I might be able to help there," Felix said. "What if we went ahead with the move, as planned, but set an ambush for the Black Fox and our delightful cousin?"

They couldn't settle their plans immediately. Joselyn would need to bring in the farmer's wives who, with Betsy the housekeeper, were her chief lieutenants. And Felix needed the officers of the troops who awaited his orders in the nearby town.

"I'll send messengers," Joselyn said.

"We can't risk Cyril finding out," Felix warned. "Is there somewhere else we can meet?"

Joselyn and her supporters fixed him with identical expressions of exasperation. "We have a place," Joselyn said patiently. "I will give your officers the direction."

The servants went to carry out Joselyn's orders, but Felix lingered, and so did Joselyn. Betsy, the last to leave, looked at her mistress uncertainly.

"Go, Betsy," Joselyn told her. "I will just have a word with Lord Maddox and be along shortly."

But when they were alone, she was silent. Was she shy, all of the sudden, his brave Joselyn?

On the clifftop, she had referred to the last time they'd seen one another; that long-ago morning when his mother had carried him off to the other end of England. Should he start there?

"Joselyn," he said. "I came back to redeem my promise."

Joselyn laughed, her mouth turning up in a smile, but something unreadable in her eyes.

"No, you did not, Felix. You came back to catch the Black Fox." And then, suddenly sober, "After eight years of silence, Felix. Eight years!"

All his excellent reasons for staying away turned to dust on his tongue in face of the angry tears pouring down her cheeks. In a moment, he had her in his arms, and was kissing the tears away, murmuring apologies and endearments.

Finally, they drew a little apart. "I have made your shoulder damp," Joselyn said, brushing at it ineffectually.

"We had better join the others, my love," Felix said. "We have a busy day ahead of us."

"Your love, Felix? You hardly know me. And I am still angry with you," she continued sternly. "Do not think to butter me up with a few kisses."

"After the ambush, I will tell you my whole story, and make whatever penance you assign. But, yes, you are my love. Now and forever, Joselyn. Show me the way to this meeting place. We can argue later."

The planning session devolved into an argument over a different topic: first Felix against Joselyn, and then—when Joselyn convinced the others of the sense of what she said—Felix against the officers and part-time smugglers alike.

Felix did not want Joselyn taking her usual place down on the beach at the head of her women. Indeed, if Felix had his way, all of the women would be replaced with his trained soldiers.

Joselyn and her helpers agreed that the soldiers would form the main part of the workforce on the beach, disguised in skirts and concealing shawls to keep their masculine features from giving away the ambush. But, Joselyn insisted, she needed to be there, head uncovered and face seen, so the villains would believe they had her trapped. And her supporters insisted on joining her.

She was right. Felix knew she was right. He hated placing her in danger, but she was essential to the success of the plan.

Reluctantly, he had to agree.

By the time Cyril returned from his errand, all was prepared. Tonight, they would trap the Black Fox.

Cyril clearly expected an outcome much more to his liking. He could hardly contain his glee when both Joselyn and Felix claimed weariness early in the evening and retired to bed. They had to hastily conceal themselves behind trees when he came crashing noisily down the path towards the clifftops, muttering to himself about tonight being the last night.

Reaching the clifftops themselves, they watched him hurry away down the path towards the village.

"I don't want you going down there, Joselyn," Felix told her. He wasn't going to stop her. She had as much at stake as he—more, given her love for these people. But he wanted her to know he was reluctant.

Had she been this frightened for him, knowing he had gone to war? If so, he'd have to spend the next fifty years making up for his unthinking cruelty in staying away so long. He smiled at the thought of that, and she smiled back.

"I will be careful. And if the smugglers come this way, you will be in more danger than I."

At that moment, the Black Fox split his forces and attacked from the sea, as well as the clifftop. For a few minutes, Felix was too busy to worry about Joselyn, but once the thugs on the clifftop were subdued, Cyril among them, he hurried down the path to the beach, where clumps of people wrestled in the moonlight.

As he reached the sand, a sudden loud shout stopped him in his tracks. "I have the woman, and I'll kill her if you try to stop me."

It was the Black Fox, his arm around Joselyn's neck, brandishing a pistol in his other hand. He was backing towards a rowboat, two of his henchmen flanking him.

"Not another step!" the Fox shrieked, as the soldiers followed him. The rest of his crew were gone, subdued by the soldiers or Joselyn's women. But no one dared approach these three.

Felix's heart was in his throat, blocking his breath and pounding like the French cannon at Waterloo. He couldn't attack without risking Joselyn, but if he didn't stop them, they'd take her with them to who-knew-what horrid fate.

The impasse was broken by a loud caw. Immediately, and so fast Felix couldn't afterward untangle the order, a large, black, feathery missile hurled itself into the Black Fox's face, Joselyn gave a twist and vicious upward punch into a portion of the Fox's anatomy that made Felix wince, two shots rang out, and the two henchmen fell.

Within seconds, it was all over, the smugglers captured and the raven marching up and down the beach, cackling with satisfaction at its own timely intervention.

Felix, with difficulty, restrained himself from wrapping Joselyn in his arms in front of half his tenants and all his soldiers. He'd never been so frightened in all his life. Thank God she was safe!

The Black Fox was hauled off into custody, along with his surviving men, and Cyril, his co-conspirator. They would face the magistrate on the morrow.

Joselyn and Felix walked home together through the dawn. The raven had flown off about his own affairs, and Joselyn's two lieutenants had gone on ahead, the housekeeper arm in arm with the farmer's wife.

"Joselyn," Felix said, "I have explanations to make—and excuses. I let everyone think I was dead because that was the best way I could serve in the war against Napoleon, but I didn't think about how it would affect you. Dare I hope you will forgive me? I will spend a lifetime making amends, if you will permit."

Joselyn was silent for a long time. He was wrong then. He had hoped she was beginning to like the adult him, at least a little.

Eventually, she spoke. "You seem very certain we would suit."

"I know we would suit," he said. "Certainly, you suit me. I did not think there was a woman in the world who so combined courage, intelligence, and spirit with beauty and kindness. I wish for a chance to convince you I can make you happy. May I court you, Joselyn?"

She was silent again, but a quality in the silence gave him hope, and he waited patiently.

"I did not know there was a man in the world who valued spirit and intelligence in a woman. I have not before met a man who would allow me to lead my troops into battle, even though he wished to protect me."

"I didn't want you to go," Felix admitted.

"But you respected me enough to agree," she said, then fell silent again.

After a while, she said, "I daresay, now that my last surviving relative is dead, my trustees will find me somewhere else to live. I cannot, of course, stay here as a unmarried woman, in the house of a bachelor to whom I am not related."

That was true, Felix supposed, his heart sinking. He hadn't thought of that. *Would she leave him, then?*

"I never knew... Felix, you really do want me, don't you? Not just my money?"

"Joselyn, I've not taken my officer's pay in eight years, and it has all been soundly invested, along with my prizes. Believe me, you are the treasure I want, not your money." He moved to take her back into his arms, but Joselyn stopped him with her hand.

"Then I wonder," she looked down shyly, "if you would consider marrying me first, Felix, and courting me after?"

So it was that Joselyn Bellingham and Felix Maddox were wed as soon as the banns could be called. If there were some who questioned the sudden change in viscounts, and wondered at the reappearance of one who had been thought dead these six years, the older servants and villagers soon put them right. If some said the bride should not have lived in the groom's house that last fortnight, Viscountess Maddox's supporters told them to hush their mouths. And if some raised their eyebrows when the bride was escorted down the aisle by a large raven, Viscount Maddox didn't care a jot. After all, he said, the raven had both found and saved his bride, and that was all there was to that.

THE END

All That Glisters

The setting is New Zealand in the 1860s, when gold miners poured into the fledgling settlement of Dunedin. Rose is unhappy in the household of her fanatical uncle, but Thomas, a young merchant from Canada, offers a glimpse of another possible life, if she is brave enough to reach for it. (Short story)

One

Rose was late. She'd been shocked, when she emerged from the Athenaeum, at how dark the sky was—her aunt would soon be looking for her to serve dinner. Rose had set a pot roast of beef on the back of the stove this morning, with the vegetables tucked around the meat, and she'd shelled the peas, too, before running Aunt Agnes' messages and stealing a little time for herself.

The Athenaeum was paradise. A subscription library and reading room at the Mechanics Institute, it provided warmth, books, and a peaceful place to read as much as she liked. And even books to take home, if she kept them hidden.

Scraping together the subscription to the Athenaeum each quarter meant sitting late over the sewing with which she earned a few extra shillings, most of which Aunt Agnes took 'to help pay for your keep, child'. As if her constant work, saving them the cost of at least one servant, were not sufficient to earn her food and a roof over her head.

She skirted around the Octagon, where the would-be millionaires flooding into the New Zealand gold fields had set up a squatters' camp with the blessing of the Dunedin Town Board. Down George Street next, thinking of her aunt, struggling to control her unchristian resentment, ignoring the drizzle and the sharp wind that wrapped her long cloak around her legs and billowed her petticoats out in front of her. As she turned the corner into Frederick St., a particularly sharp gust skittered a broken branch across her path, tangling it into her skirts.

She stumbled and would have landed in the mud, if firm hands had not suddenly caught her. As it was, in putting her hands out to break the expected fall, she had dropped her burdens. The shopping basket fell sideways, tumbling fruit, vegetables, and the wrapped parcel of meat into a waiting puddle. The bundle from the haberdashers that she carried on her other arm, thankfully, stayed intact and landed on a relatively dry spot.

She took all this in at a glance, most of her attention on her rescuer. A craggy face bronzed by the sun, amused brown eyes under thick, level brows, a mouth that looked made for laughter. He was bundled against the cold wind in a greatcoat, muffler, and cloth cap.

"Are you all right, Miss?" the man asked, as he set her back on her feet.

My. He was strong.

"Thank you. The branch… Oh, dear, my parcels!" He crouched with her to rescue tomorrow's roast, now peeping through tears in the soggy brown paper. He looked doubtfully at a particularly dirty carrot and wiped it off on a handkerchief he pulled from his pocket.

"Oh, no," Rose said, as he started to put her damp groceries back in the basket. She retrieved the book she had hidden there, tucking it inside her coat so it would stay dry. Her rescuer made no comment, just continued helping her fill the basket.

"That seems to be the lot," he said, bringing back an apple that had rolled a good distance along the path, and picking up the basket. "Which way now?"

Rose ignored the proffered elbow. "I can manage, thank you, Sir. If you would just give me my basket…"

He grinned, showing white, even teeth. "I must insist. Damsels in distress do not land in a knight errant's hands every day, you know. I shall, at least, escort you safely to your front door, fair maiden."

"You may not, Sir." He really couldn't. If a man escorted her to the front door, or even to her uncle's front gate, it would be fasting and prayer for her, and perhaps even the switch. She set her mouth firmly to stop it from trembling, but he must have sensed her alarm, because he handed over the basket without further argument.

"There, now. No need to be concerned. I mean no harm, Miss."

She was blushing again; she could feel the heat. The kindness in his eyes was as appealing as his strength and his cheeky smile.

"I cannot," she found herself explaining. "My uncle… he would be angry…"

He nodded as if he understood. "I will bid you good evening then, Miss. But before I go, can you help a poor, lost traveller and point me in the direction of Knox Lane?"

"Knox Lane?" she repeated, stupidly.

"Yes. Do you know it?"

"I live there," Rose said. It was a short cul-de-sac, with only three houses besides her uncle's. She looked at the man more closely, wondering which of her neighbours he intended to visit.

"Then, Miss, will you not reconsider your decision and allow me to escort you? I can leave you at the corner of this elusive lane, so you need have no fear, and it would be a charitable act to a poor traveller." He made a woebegone face, turning the corners of his mouth down with his lips poked out, wrinkling his brow, so his brows sank at the side and rose in the centre.

Rose smiled despite herself, and surrendered the basket to his waiting hand. "Just to the corner then, Sir."

"Allow me to introduce myself," he said, as they turned the next corner and walked briskly along Great King Street, pushed by the wind. "I am Thomas O'Bryan, from America."

Ah. She had been wondering about his accent. Beyond a doubt, he was another of the great army of men passing through Dunedin on their way to the gold fields at Tuapeka or Dunstan. Fools. Yes, a few of them would find a rich deposit, but most would abandon their families and their responsibilities and return, if return they ever did, with nothing. Rose knew only too well what became of those left behind.

"Rose Campbell." Her thoughts tinged her voice with ice, and he raised one of those mobile brows. "Campbell?" he repeated. "Do not be telling me, of all the women in New Zealand, I've collided with Agnes Campbell's daughter."

"Her niece," Rose corrected. "You know my aunt?"

O'Bryan grinned, a joyous beam that invited her to find life as delightful as he clearly did. "Not to say know, but isn't she my own mother's sister?" He bowed, an extravagant flourish. "How do you do, Cousin Rose."

"Not exactly a cousin, Mr O'Bryan," Rose demurred. "Your aunt is married to my uncle."

"Thomas, surely? For cousins so closely related by marriage?"

"Laura!" Rose could not help the guilty flinch at the accusing roar from her uncle. Thomas stepped in front of her, and held out his hand with another of his broad grins. "Do I have the honour of addressing my Uncle Campbell?" he asked.

The sour, old man ignored Thomas' hand, but turned his glower away from the cowering girl, which Thomas counted as a win. "Who are you, and what are you doing with my niece?"

"Thomas O'Bryan, sir, and I believe I am your nephew-by-marriage. I was asking the young lady for directions."

"Agnes' nephew." The thought clearly did not find favour. "I suppose you're here after the gold, like all those other godless sinners. Well, you had better come in." The old coot turned to lead the way down the street, saying over his shoulder, "Laura, I'll speak with you later, girl."

Thomas gave his new cousin a reassuring wink, but she dipped her head and hurried after the domestic tyrant.

Thomas' aunt proved to be cut from the same cloth as her husband, and as far from Thomas' cheerful mother as could be imagined. She reluctantly allowed that Thomas could stay to dinner, and swept off towards the back of the house, chivvying the niece ahead of her.

"No time to waste mooning in your room, Laura. We'll need to put on more potatoes to stretch the stew. Put those bundles away..." A closing door shut off the detail of Aunt Agnes' tirade, but not the sound of her scold, pitched at a droning whine that set Thomas' teeth on edge.

"Where do you stay this night?" the old man demanded.

Thomas had assumed he would be resisting an invitation to stay here. In Canada, where he was raised, his parents found room for any traveller, let alone a hitherto unknown nephew. In San Francisco, where his business partner lived, the same habits prevailed. Thomas had already taken rooms at the Empire Hotel, but he was surprised not to be offered a bed here.

Campbell made the wrong assumption from his silence. "There's a camp. In the middle of town. Those heading for the gold fields can find tent space."

So he'd be given dinner then turned out into the night. And leave without any regrets, except that he'd like to know a little more about his cousin-by-marriage.

"So they told me when I arrived, Sir," he said, perversely not wishing to let this poor excuse for an uncle know he had already arranged his own accommodation

He continued to make attempts at conversation, each one squashed by Campbell, until they were called to dinner. The table, in the second front room, sharing space with a pair of fireside chairs, a large roll-top desk, and a treadle sewing machine, had been moved far enough from the wall to allow the use of four of the six wooden chairs. Aunt Agnes brought a platter of fresh sliced bread, while Miss Campbell carried in a large pot and returned for another.

After a long prayer of thanksgiving that sounded more like a diatribe against persons unnamed, Campbell gestured them to sit. So began one of the most uncomfortable meals of Thomas' life.

The stew was delicious, if somewhat sparse. Thomas dug into the bread with enthusiasm to fill the gaps.

"My mother sends her love," Thomas said, a little mendaciously. Mama had actually told him, *I suppose you had better visit Agnes, though I don't suppose you'll be welcomed.*

This conversational opener fetched a contemptuous harrumph from Campbell, and a nod of acknowledgement from Aunt Agnes.

Thomas tried again. "The stew is delicious. My compliments." He nodded to his aunt, but it was Miss Campbell who murmured thanks, sliding frightened eyes sideways to her uncle.

What now? The weather? Ladies' fashions? Greek history? Stargazing or birdwatching? Did nobody at this benighted table talk over dinner?

Before he could make a comment on the beauty of the long Otago Harbour inlet, Aunt Agnes surprised him by asking, "How is my sister?"

"Well, Ma'am, she was well when I left San Francisco. She is staying with my sister, Catherine, to help with the older children, while my sister is lying in with the new baby."

"Three children is it, now?" Aunt Agnes asked, her tone softening, and something like longing in her eyes.

"Yes. Two boys, and now a little girl. Cath and Patrick are delighted."

"More half-breed, Papist idolaters bound for Hell," Mr Campbell grumbled, seemingly to his plate. Thomas controlled the urge to retaliate in kind. Campbell had clearly not softened since the days when his mother and her sister, two good, Presbyterian girls in Edinburgh, were being courted. Both married and emigrated. Mother had gone with her merry husband to Canada, where she was welcomed by his Irish father and his mother's large Métis clan, descendants of a French trapper and his Cree wife. Aunt Agnes and her dour non-conformist chose to move far from all they knew to New Zealand, where they moved from one congregation to another until he invented one strict enough for his tastes.

Aunt Agnes, who had been about to say something more, subsided. Another conversational sally cut off at the pass.

"I thought your harbour very beautiful," Thomas offered. "The hills either side... it is very like parts of the west coast of Canada, where I grew up."

Miss Campbell looked as if she might reply, but clearly thought better of it, and neither of the others said a word.

In the end, Thomas gave up and simply ate his meal. Another interminable Grace in place of dessert was clearly a signal that dinner was over, and Aunt Agnes and Miss Campbell began to clear.

Thomas stood when they rose. "May I pay my guest gift by helping with the dishes?" he asked.

Campbell answered for the women. "The girls will do it. My niece and the maid. Women's work."

Thomas, who had fended for himself in a long succession of miner's towns, where women were few and far between, once again swallowed his opinion. The evening would soon be over, and he could escape.

Sooner than he thought, it appeared. "Agnes, fetch the boy's coat," the old man commanded, and Aunt Agnes scurried to obey.

"Thank you for dinner, Ma'am," Thomas said. "Mama will be pleased to know I found you well."

Aunt Agnes handed him his coat with one hand, and waved Miss Campbell's book with the other. "Look what I found under the coats, Mr Campbell. That girl has been reading again!"

Miss Campbell had returned to the room to finish clearing the table, and stood behind her uncle, transfixed, her face white.

"My book!" Thomas exclaimed. "It must have fallen out of my pocket."

Aunt Agnes looked at him, doubtfully, but handed him the book, and Campbell shut the mouth that had been open to roar. "And what is that you're reading?" he grumbled, frowning.

Thomas, who had no idea of the answer, held the book up so Campbell could see the embossed title for himself.

"*Dombey and Son*. That Charles Dickens fellow. Rubbish."

Thomas tucked the book into his pocket, shook Campbell's hand, thanked him for his hospitality (may his lips not shrivel—two lies in as many minutes!), and gave his aunt a dutiful salute on a cold, papery cheek.

Miss Campbell had faded from the room again, silent as a ghost. No matter. As the front door closed behind him, Thomas ducked along in front of the parlour window and down the narrow path at the side of the house to the lean-to scullery at the rear.

Miss Campbell was bent over the sink, while another girl dried each dish as it was handed to her. He waited, watching through the window, as they completed the dishes, and then continued to wait some more.

He doubted that Campbell, the nasty old miser, let them burn candles sitting up late. Before long, each of them would make the journey down the path to the outhouse at the foot of the garden. With luck, he could return Miss Campbell her book with no one else the wiser.

Within half an hour, his expectation was fulfilled, as first the maid, then Campbell himself, then Aunt Agnes made the trip. When it was Miss Campbell's turn with the lantern, he waited until she returned and spoke from the shadows, keeping his voice soft, so as not to alarm her.

"Miss Campbell, I waited to return your book."

Clever girl. She kept her eyes on the back door, but slowed her steps, saying quietly, "Aunt Agnes is watching. I will be back shortly to collect wood. The wood pile is beyond that shed." She indicated with her head, still not looking at him.

"I will be there," Thomas told her. He kept to the shadows, but was in place to meet her when she carried out a basket to fill with wood for the morning fire.

"Maisie will be here in a moment, Mr O'Bryan, to help me carry the basket back inside. Thank you for telling Uncle Campbell it was your book."

"Here you are, Miss Campbell." He handed her the book, and she slipped it inside the waistband of her skirt, loosening, then retying, the shawl that insulated her against the chill night air.

A clatter of wooden pattens heralded the arrival of the maid, and Thomas faded into the darkness, leaving the two of them to their task.

He sauntered back along George Street to his hotel. He could write to his Mama and let her know her sister was well. He had done his duty and need not visit again. But he would not at all mind seeing Miss Campbell once more.

Two

Mr O'Bryan was a bright spot in an otherwise dismal week. Rose's lateness returning home that night had been overshadowed by the American nephew's crimes of being a Papist, a gold miner, and an uninvited dinner guest. She escaped with no more than an extra fifteen minutes on her knees, and the linen closet to turn out. She managed to read the book Mr O'Bryan had saved for her in the week before it was due for return, keeping it in her apron pocket, stealing moments at the clothesline or in the kitchen when Aunt Agnes was occupied with the ladies' church committee.

On Thursday, Mr Hackerton came to dinner. A widower and an elder at the Congregation of the Elect meetinghouse, he was looking Rose over for her potential as a wife and housekeeper. Rose shuddered. Imagine: a lifetime of being called 'Laura', and being touched by those cold, pudgy hands.

On Saturday, the entire house had to be cleaned from top to bottom, and the next day's food cooked, so the day could be spent in prayer and meditation, when not at one of two long church services conducted by Uncle Campbell and the other elders.

And on Monday, she saw Thomas O'Bryan again. She was coming back from shopping, nervously skirting the noisy camp in the Octagon, when he materialised beside her, tipped his cap, and held out a hand for her basket.

"Let me carry that for you, Miss Campbell. It looks heavy." He fell into step, saying cheerfully, "As I thought. Far too heavy for a little bit of a thing like yourself."

"I thought you would have gone to the fields by now, Mr O'Bryan," she said.

"There now, you have been thinking of me!" Something in his grin made her insides feel peculiar, and she looked away, feeling the heat rise in her face.

"I have business to attend to in Dunedin, but I've passage booked on the coach tomorrow," he explained. "And what are we shopping for, this fine, crisp, spring morning?" He lifted the corner of a package, and shifted another sideways, ignoring her anxious fluttering. "Is there another book concealed beneath the potatoes, Miss Campbell?"

"Don't say that," she darted her eyes about, hoping no one who knew her uncle had overheard. They were all strangers, intent on their own affairs, and Mr O'Bryan was regarding her with chagrin.

"I was only teasing, Miss Campbell. No one heard, and your secrets are safe with me. The old crow and his wife object to you reading?"

She flushed to hear her secret description for her nearest living relations on the lips of this irreverent man, but something about his clear interest tugged a murmured admission from her. "Uncle says the Bible is the only proper reading for a pious woman."

"Which bits?" Mr O'Bryan enquired with interest. "The Song of Songs? The story about Lot's daughters? Or Tamar?"

"Mr O'Bryan!" He could not possibly know of her minor rebellion, seeking out the most shocking stories she could find in the Bible, whenever her uncle set her reading.

"What?" He tried to keep his face bland, but one corner of his mouth twitched, and his eyes twinkled.

By now, they were out of the shopping area and approaching the turn into Frederick Street. "Thank you for your escort, sir," Rose told him. "I can manage from here."

"I am visiting my aunt, Miss Campbell, so I'll do myself the honour of seeing you home."

<hr />

Thomas was surprised to hear himself say so. He'd intended to steer clear of his aunt and her poisonous husband, despite his attraction to the niece. Unusual for him to be attracted to a little mouse; though, he had to admit, she had backbone, sneaking books into the house under the old man's nose. There was more to her than met the eye.

But she was all wrong for Thomas—Protestant, and puritan at that. This New Zealand venture would establish his fortune, and he'd return home to San Francisco to look for a wife—a good, Catholic girl like Mary Rourke, the daughter of his partner. Ben had hoped… and Thomas had started seriously thinking about it, but he had thought too long, and came back from a trip to Canada to find the girl betrothed—to a local farmer, of all things.

Miss Campbell was nothing like Miss Rourke. Slender, where Miss Rourke was prettily plump, quiet and contained, while Miss Rourke was vivacious and outgoing, wary, when Miss Rourke expected the world to shape itself to her command. Miss Rourke was all colour—red hair, rosy cheeks, blue-green eyes, bright gowns and shawls and bonnets. Miss Campbell was shades of brown—light hair the shade of a mouse pelt; soft, brown eyes, lightened with gold flecks; skin a pale olive, lit at the moment by the bright colour that rose so easily to her face; and her drab, serviceable, beige dress cut too large and untrimmed.

She should be dressed in green or red or a warm, rosy pink; something that would give her colour, instead of draining it. If she were his, he'd buy her colours.

Protestant, he reminded himself. Not for him.

"Why does your uncle call you 'Laura'?" he asked, to turn his mind from the subject.

"He does not like my other name," she explained.

"Rose Laura?" He tried it on his tongue. "Or Laura Rose?"

"Laura Rose, but my papa always called me Rose. Uncle says it is a Pap… Uncle does not like it."

Thomas could easily supply the word she caught back: *Papist.* Another reminder that they occupied separate worlds. "Rose is a very pretty name," he said.

She smiled, and the grim spring day became unexpectedly brighter.

"What business keeps you in Dunedin, Mr O'Bryan?"

"Mining supplies, Miss Campbell. My firm, Rourke and O'Bryan, sells supplies to miners, and I am here in New Zealand to set up supply lines and open stores in the main fields."

"Food, you mean?"

"And pans and shovels and blankets and buckets and clothing and tents… My father and his partner began the firm in California thirteen years ago, when I was a wee bit of a boy, and Ben Rourke took me into the firm when my father died."

"I am sorry for your loss, Mr O'Bryan. Is it… recent?"

"Three years ago, but I cannot seem to realise it, somehow. I was in South Australia, and by the time I received the letter telling me he was ill, he had already gone to his reward."

Thomas shook his head, grimacing. He'd returned home on the first ship that could give him passage, but arrived in Vancouver six weeks past the funeral.

His sister, Mary-Elizabeth, and her family had moved into the fine, new house his parents had built, so his mother would not be alone. But when he was home, Thomas constantly expected to be told it had all been a mistake, to see, at any moment, his father walking in through the front door, kissing his wife, tickling his grandson, and making a joke about the removal of his favourite chair to the attic, since Mama could neither bear to look at it, nor give it away.

Thomas shook off the mood. The whole family had offered Masses for the repose of Papa's soul, and Thomas had performed all the requirements for a plenary indulgence at Christmastide, on Papa's behalf, these past three years. Papa was a good man, and surely in Purgatory at least, if not in Heaven already.

"What of your own family, Miss Campbell? How do you come to be living with your aunt and uncle?"

Miss Campbell wilted, all the vitality sinking out of her, and Thomas felt an almost overpowering urge to give her a hug and bring some warmth back into her face.

"Never mind," he said, hastily. "You need not talk about it, if you do not wish."

If they turned now, they would be at the Campbell's cottage before he was ready. He deliberately continued straight ahead, and she followed meekly along, her thoughts far away.

"I do not mind," she said, breaking the silence. "The story is a short one. My mother died shortly after I was born, and my father raised me. Then, five years ago, he left me with his brother and went off to Australia. He said the gold fields were no place for a growing girl. A few months later… he drowned, Mr O'Bryan. A flash flood, they said, several miners swept away."

Thomas led her into a small patch of uncleared trees, hidden from those passing, so she need not be embarrassed by the tears pouring silently down her cheeks. He put a comforting arm on hers, and she leant into his hug, shoulders heaving as she tried to contain her sobs.

"Cry away, Miss Campbell," he told her. "I have two sisters who have cried on me more times than I can count, and no one else will ever know."

Miss Campbell shook her head, and took several deep, shuddery breaths.

"Uncle Campbell would not like me to return home red-eyed. He says my father is burning in Hell for a sinner, and I should not mourn such a man. But he was a good man, Mr O'Bryan. Always humming and telling jokes and hoping for the best. God would not be so cruel as to keep him from Heaven, just because he played the piano at dances and sometimes missed a church service. He would not, would he?"

Thomas was not qualified to give an opinion on the salvation of heretics. He hedged. "Didn't Jesus say we don't know? That some who think they are saved won't be, and some who think they are not, will be? Love counts, I think. And kindness." He hoped so, anyway, and the thought cheered Miss Campbell, who pulled back from his arms and set about tidying the bonnet she'd knocked askew against his shoulder.

How pretty she was, even with her eyes slightly puffy.

They continued walking, and to change the subject, he began telling her about the clerks he had hired and the warehouse he had rented and the store he intended to build in Hartley Township, in the Dunstan gold fields. She asked intelligent questions, entering with enthusiasm into discussion of his plans, and by the time they arrived at the Campbell's cottage, all physical signs of Miss Campbell's grief had faded.

Thomas sat through an awkward visit with his aunt, who made no effort to conceal her surprise at seeing him again, bur reluctantly offered him tea, which he drank at the kitchen table while Aunt Agnes, the maid, and Miss Campbell bustled about preparing an evening meal.

Aunt Agnes was visibly relieved when he finished the cup of weak tea and refused to stay for dinner. "Mr Campbell will be sorry to have missed you," she said.

Thomas met the lie with one of his own, sending the old bully his best wishes.

He had no more wish to sit at his aunt's meagre board than she to have him there. So why, when he took his coat and hat from Miss Campbell, did he bend closer and say, "I will do myself the honour of calling again when I am in Dunedin, Miss Campbell"?

Three

Mr O'Bryan's visits were the highlight of the month, and Dunedin felt wetter, windier, and colder after he left. Rose struggled with snail depredations and weeds in the vegetable garden, did the shopping, cooked, cleaned, sewed in the evenings, and woke earlier and earlier with the lengthening day, to read a little in the dawn light before another day of unrelenting work.

From time to time, but perhaps not more than a dozen times a day, she wondered how Mr O'Bryan was faring in Dunstan and whether he would, indeed, call on them when he returned to Dunedin.

Then, suddenly, in early December, he was there again, falling into step beside her as she walked from Knox Lane to George Street on her way shopping.

"Good morning, Miss Campbell. May I carry your basket?" He was taking it from her as he spoke, his impish grin robbing the gesture of any offence.

"You're back," Rose said. What a foolish thing to say, but her wits had taken flight at his presence.

"I am. And do I find you well?"

She stammered something, trying to collect her scattered thoughts.

"And did your business prosper, Mr O'Bryan?" she managed.

"It did, thank you. The first cartloads of goods sold before they reached Dunstan. I've taken on two more assistants for the tent store and a building to house Rourke and O'Bryan is going up in Hartley Township, as we speak. All is going well there, and so I've come to attend to business at this end of the trail."

Rose looked around her, wondering what business he found in this mainly residential area, and he must have guessed her thoughts, because he said, "Today, I am taking an afternoon's holiday. I was on my way to visit you when, behold, here you are walking toward me. Dare I hope to escort you the entire afternoon, Miss Campbell?"

She smiled her consent, all at once feeling giddy. But someone might see them and report to her uncle! Well, what of it? She would still have the memory of the afternoon—a little treasure to take out and enjoy when he was gone, and she was alone.

He threw himself into the shopping with enthusiasm, debating the merits of various meats, solemnly inspecting vegetables, giving his view on the best threads to match and contrast with the cushion cover she was decorating.

When she hesitated over some bonnet trimmings, yearning for a confection of silk flowers and feathers, he offered to buy them. She blushed at the scandalous suggestion, but was not as displeased as she should be.

"No, indeed, Mr O'Bryan. My uncle would never allow me to wear any bonnet they would make. I will have three yards of the brown ribbon, please," she told the assistant.

Mr O'Bryan subsided, but his next suggestion was that they should take tea at the Empire Hotel. Rose hesitated. Anyone might walk together when out shopping, but to take tea with a man at his hotel was surely a wanton act. Or so her uncle would say, in any case.

At that moment, they passed Hackerton's Emporium, and even from the footpath, she could hear the man her uncle intended her to wed berating an unfortunate employee.

"Very well, Mr O'Bryan," she said. Another memory to cherish. Why not?

She had passed the tea rooms at the Empire on several occasions, but never thought to enter. She felt very grand sitting at one of their white-linen-covered tables, with a tiered cake plate of toothsome delicacies and a dainty china cup full of fragrant tea. And a handsome, charming, attentive escort, who kept her entertained with stories of people in the burgeoning boomtown at the Dunstan.

She was very much in charity with him as they made their way back up Princes Street and through the Octagon, skirting the muddy centre, where the churning population of miners briefly settled, before heading up the Dunstan trail to Central Otago.

In the next moment, her contentment took a knock.

"Mr O'Bryan!" The speaker was a tall, striking-looking woman with bold, dark eyes and porcelain skin, set off to perfection by her black dress and bonnet. In the next moment, Rose realised that the veil, currently pushed back from the perfect oval of the woman's face, marked her a widow. She was older than Rose had thought at first, too—older than Thom... Mr O'Bryan, that was certain.

"Mr O'Bryan, I want to thank you, Sir. The money has been—I cannot tell you. All those sharks that hovered after the money Arthur owed them..." The woman shuddered.

"Payment for services rendered, Mrs Moffat, and for those you have promised me. And how is little Mary? Better, I hope? Oh, but I forget my manners. Miss Campbell, allow me to present Mrs Moffat, who works for me. Mrs Moffat, Miss Campbell is my cousin."

The woman gave Rose a distracted nod and a brief curtsey before hurrying on, "I must get back to her. I just popped out for a few groceries and left young Arthur in charge, and Mary will not mind him when she is fretful. But I am grateful for it, Mr O'Bryan, for if she is fretful, she is on the mend, so the doctor says. And we will be in Hartley Township in the new year, I promise you that, Sir."

"Whenever the little girl is well enough, Mrs Moffat. You are not to be anxious about it."

The widow said her farewells, repeating her thanks, and hurried off, with Rose looking thoughtfully after her.

"A sad case, Miss Campbell. Her husband managed the warehouse I am leasing here in Dunedin, or so I thought. But a fortnight ago, he walked off the end of the wharf and drowned, leaving a wife and seven little ones."

"Oh, how terrible!" Rose was berating herself for her uncharitable thoughts.

"When I arrived, I found the warehouse humming along nicely, and it transpired that Mrs Moffat has been running it all along, while Moffat drank his income. I'd leave her in charge, but some of the ships' captains won't deal with a woman, so I offered her management of the store in Hartley Township."

"That was very generous of you."

"Not really. The miners behave better with a woman than a man, and—to be very selfish about it—she is old enough and soured enough on marriage not to be stolen to the altar almost before she arrives at the fields."

"You paid her husband's debts," Rose guessed, "and probably the doctor's bill, too." She smiled at him. What a kind man he was.

⋘⋙

And the rent through to the end of January, Thomas thought, but couldn't bring himself to say, a little embarrassed at Rose's obvious approval. *Just good business.* He needed a reliable, loyal storekeeper, and the price he'd paid to redeem Moffat's gambling debts and pay his bills was cheap, compared to bringing someone of his own from another continent.

And Miss Campbell's smile upon hearing the tale was a bonus; a lovely, joyful, open beam that transformed the dismal day into glorious summer.

Before he recovered from the mind-reeling effects of it, he found himself inviting her to the Grand Ball in January, being held by the Committee of the Widows and Orphans Institution of the Oddfellows. Just like that, the sun went out.

"Freemasonry is the work of the devil, and dancing encourages licentious behaviour," she told him, primly, but her eyes were wistful.

"It will be a subscription assembly conducted by ladies of the highest probity," Thomas assured her. "Do say you will come, Miss Campbell."

"I cannot." The wistfulness leaked into her voice. "Uncle Campbell would never allow it."

They were at Campbell's front door, and he could say no more, not wishing to draw the ire of Aunt Agnes upon her vulnerable head.

Aunt Agnes was no more welcoming than she had been the last time, making a few minutes of desultory conversation before reluctantly offering him a cup of tea, which he enthusiastically refused, claiming the pressure of other business.

"But I could not be at this end of town without paying my respects, Ma'am," he said, his tongue firmly in his cheek.

After Aunt Agnes had seen him off at the front door, he doubled back to slip between the narrow houses to the rear garden, where Rose was struggling with the wind to pull in a line of sheets and other linen.

Without a word, Thomas came to her aid, his extra height helping him reach the pegs easily and fold the sheets more quickly.

Again, he was rewarded by a softening in her fine eyes, and that bright smile. "Thank you. Mostly, it is not a problem, but when the wind gets up, I swear the washing has a mind of its own! At least it is not wet."

She folded the personal items he had politely left for her to retrieve, and tucked them under the sheets in the wash basket. How pretty she looked, embarrassment touching her cheeks with the rose of her name.

"The dance is on the sixth of January," he said.

"I know."

"I will be back in Dunedin by Christmas, or not long after. If you will trust me, Cousin Rose, I'll come and fetch you for the dance and make sure you get back safely."

"I cannot." Her eyes yearned, but her voice was firm. "My uncle would never permit it. And it would be wrong of me to disobey him while I live under his roof."

"If you change your mind, a message at the Empire Hotel will reach me," he told her. But he didn't press her any further. He should be grateful she refused him. No good could come of such an evening, however innocent.

It was an afternoon to pack away in her memories, and pull out to relive again and again. Rose had to be careful not to hum as she prepared and served dinner. Even listening to her uncle's lectures and instructions over the meal could not suppress her mood entirely, nor did facing the pile of dishes that needed to be washed before she could go to bed, this being the maid's half-day.

As she washed and dried, she imagined what it might be like to attend the Grand Ball. Now that would be a memory to treasure!

Rose packed away the dishes, scrubbed the sink, and set some oats to soften overnight for breakfast porridge, all the time, listing in her head the many reasons why accepting Mr O'Bryan's invitation would be disastrous.

She believed him when he said there would be no harm in it. Why, even in their small break-away congregation, with its strict rules about social behaviour, some of the other women were going to the event. One was even on the organising committee!

But Uncle disapproved, and so she could not think of it.

Four

But the idea would not go away, and as Christmas rushed ever nearer, Rose nerved herself to approach her uncle and ask if she might go to the ball. She did not even have time to confess to Mr O'Bryan's invitation before he gave her an indignant refusal, followed with two hours of writing, in her best hand, the admonishments from the letters of St Paul about the behaviour of women.

She had expected nothing else, but that did not prevent her despondency. She was disappointed, too, as the Christmas Octave began, and Mr O'Bryan did not appear. She scanned the streets as she shopped, negotiating the excited crowds and looking wistfully at seasonal decorations.

The Campbell household did not celebrate the feast, except with an extra-long church service. No special preparations, no decorations, no presents.

Watching Mrs Moffat and two of her children negotiating with the grocer for baking supplies, arguing about which particular treats they would make, gave her a pang. She and her father used to bake special cakes and other treats at Christmas. They had hung ribbons and greenery to decorate the house, and sung carols together each evening. Christmas day had meant a special meal, and little gifts made or purchased in secret and presented to each other with great delight. At Christmas, more than ever, she missed him.

Mrs Moffat recognised her and stopped to say hello, admonishing the children to stand still or they'd have no treats, nor presents either, perhaps. They grinned, not at all concerned, but waited patiently nonetheless, while Rose asked after the sick child. "She is on the mend, thank the Virgin and all the saints," Mrs Moffat said. "We will be following Mr O'Bryan up to Dunstan in a few weeks; by the end of January, beyond a doubt. And have you heard from the dear man, Miss Campbell?"

Rose shook her head. "He said he hoped to be back in Dunedin before, or just after, Christmas, which is only a few days away."

"Well, if ever the world held a man who keeps his word, it is Mr O'Bryan. An angel from Heaven, he has been to me and mine. Don't think I cannot see you poking your brother, Margaret Moffat. Butter would not melt in her mouth, that one, Miss Campbell, but I have to watch her every minute. I had best be getting them off home, and leave you to do your shopping. Merry Christmas."

Rose wished the same to Mrs Moffat and the children. She expected they would have a happier Christmas than she. It would take more than the kind of miracle Mr O'Bryan had wrought for the Moffat family, to turn Aunt Agnes and Uncle Campbell into Christmas carollers.

Christmas Day was even worse than expected. No Mr O'Bryan, and too much Mr Hackerton. He came home with the Campbells after church and stayed for dinner, and Rose had to endure him and Uncle Campbell discussing her cooking and housekeeping skills, as if she were a piece of merchandise whose purchase Mr Hackerton was considering. Which, of course, she was.

As she and Maisie cleaned up after the meal, she listened to the maid's grumbles with half her attention, much of her focus on whether she could refuse Mr Hackerton's courtship, and what her uncle would do if she did.

Maisie's chatter penetrated her distraction. "… leaving at the end of the quarter, and so I told him. 'I am not your niece, to be kept from any fun and work for nothing every day of the week without a holiday,' I told him."

Maisie was leaving? "But what will you do? Where will you go?"

Maisie scoffed. "Oh, Miss, with servants taking off after gold, and all the new people, there is plenty of work for a willing girl. I don't have to stay where they won't give me a half-day at Christmas. No, I'll see out the quarter, but come 31 December, when my wages is due, I'm taking my leave, and so I have told Mr and Mrs Campbell." She nodded, her lips pursed in satisfaction. "Yes, and you should do the same, Miss."

She should, too. The seed, thus planted, rapidly took root. Plenty of work, was there? It couldn't be harder than she did here. Indeed, the difference between the way the Campbells treated their niece and the way they treated their servant put all the benefits on Maisie's side—wages, a half-day a week off, as well as time to attend the church services of her choice.

Rose would be twenty-one on the thirtieth of January, no longer under her uncle's guardianship.

She began to question Maisie about how one went about finding a job.

⊹⊱≺≻⊰⊹

Rose, full of her own plans for a future in domestic service, was completely taken by surprise when Uncle Campbell announced, a few days before the sixth of January, that he had given his approval for Mr Hackerton to escort her to the Grand Ball for the benefit of the Widows and Orphans.

She was torn. On the one hand, she had no desire to encourage Mr Hackerton's courtship. On the other, this might be her only opportunity to attend such an event. Then again, she had nothing fit to wear to a ball. But that hardly mattered, did it? She would be there to see all the beautiful gowns and enjoy the music, so what she wore was of no importance.

With all these ideas cluttering up her tongue, she could only stammer, "The Ball, Uncle?"

"Hackerton thinks it will be a treat for you, and I've said you will go, Laura, so go you shall."

Rose nodded her acquiescence, and went up to lay her Sunday-best gown out on the bed. It was brown, a soft, mousy colour, a shade or two darker than her hair. Plain, cut high to the neck and loose in the waist, it was not flattering. But it was serviceable, and it was what she had. She sighed and returned it to its hook.

When she had wages, she would buy herself a Sunday dress in green, or perhaps blue. And flowers and ribbons to trim her bonnets. As she came downstairs to answer a knock on the door, she smiled at the thought.

Maisie was right about the dearth of servants; Aunt Agnes was finding it hard to replace the maid, and would not be happy at all when Rose left. Her smile broadened at the thought, and she was grinning when she opened the door.

There on the step stood Thomas O'Bryan.

Miss Campbell met Thomas with a happy smile, and for a moment, all he could do was smile back.

She recalled him to himself, saying, "Why, it is Mr O'Bryan! Come in, Sir. Are you here to see your aunt?"

I am here to see you, Rose, he wanted to say, but he kept his peace and followed her to the parlour where Aunt Agnes sat at a narrow desk, writing out accounts.

"Turned up again, have you?" Aunt Agnes said, but though the words sounded unenthusiastic, she surprised him with a smile that was almost welcoming.

Thomas pulled out the first of the presents with which he had armed himself. "Happy Christmas, Aunt Agnes."

"We do not celebrate Christmas in this house, young man." Campbell had been sitting, unnoticed, on a chair facing away from the door. His glower followed his voice as he rose to glare at Thomas.

"Happy New Year then, Uncle," Thomas said, peaceably, handing the old man a package wrapped in brown paper and tied with string, and passing another to Aunt Agnes.

For a moment, the two hesitated, then curiosity and avarice overcame their distaste, and they both began to untie the string.

Thomas turned to give his third present—the reason he'd bothered to bring the other two—to Rose, but she had left the room, and he had to wait.

Aunt Agnes thanked him for the pretty shawl, and Campbell, with considerably less grace, grumbled his grudging appreciation of the pen-and-wiper set.

"Take a seat, if you are staying. I suppose that girl has gone to make tea," Campbell said. Thomas sat, determined to remain until he could speak to Rose.

Almost immediately, he stood again, and hurried to help her with a heavy tray.

"Thank you, Mr O'Bryan." She blushed as he took the tray from her, and would have left the room again, had he not spoken.

"Miss Campbell, I trust I see you well?"

"Yes, thank you, Mr O'Bryan."

Campbell interrupted, frowning. "No point in making calf's eyes at my niece, boy. I'm supposing it is her you have rushed to see, all the way from Dunstan."

"I came to bring you presents, Uncle, as I said. I am a few days later than I intended," Thomas apologised. "I told you I would be here just after Christmas, Aunt Agnes, and that's more than a week past. But here I am now.

"I have a present for Miss Campbell, as well." He handed Rose the wrapped parcel, and her eyes shone when she found a duplicate to the shawl he had given Aunt Agnes, but with green the dominant colour, rather than the deep, wine red he had chosen for his aunt.

Campbell looked even dourer. He clearly wanted to complain, but could not, having accepted his own gift.

"So what kept you, Thomas?" Aunt Agnes wanted to know.

"I thought I had sufficient time to visit the new fields, Aunt Agnes." He studiously did not look at Rose, for whom he intended the explanation. "Up on the Arrow and the Wakatip, they're making finds every day, and at least one new town will be needed, perhaps more. Certainly, Hartley Township is too far for the diggers to bring their gold and buy supplies." The new town would have a Rourke and O'Bryan store for those diggers to patronise. He had already purchased the land and hired the builders, though that wasn't the whole reason for the delay.

No need to tell the ladies he'd discovered a body in the river— some poor digger drowned in the winter, by the looks of it, his remains exposed as the water level dropped. Rose, in particular, did not need to know he'd had to stay up the Arrow to give evidence at the inquest.

Might as well take the bull by the horns and address his real reason for coming. "Uncle, I hoped to gain your permission to escort Miss Campbell to the Grand Ball. It is for a good cause, and will be a gentile event."

Campbell opened his mouth, but Aunt Agnes spoke first. "You are too late, Thomas. Laura has an escort. A gentleman from our congregation."

"It is a respectable event, and her escort has my approval." Campbell got to his feet. "Laura. Mrs Campbell. You'll be about your work, if you please. I'll be having a word with O'Bryan here."

The ladies, Rose looking anxiously over her shoulder, left the room, and Thomas listened politely to the not-unexpected lecture from Campbell. He was to leave Miss Campbell alone. He was the wrong religion for her, and too worldly, and altogether unsuitable. Campbell had chosen her husband, and Thomas was not to interfere in any way, up to and including visiting her, dancing with her, and speaking to her.

Thomas said very little, seeing no point in causing trouble for Rose by arguing. Besides, Campbell's objections were the same he'd raised for himself. They came from different worlds, he and Rose.

But somehow, hearing Campbell say it made him want to defend what he and Rose had in common. Whatever it was that was growing between them, if it proved to be real and true, could stand a bit of difference, surely? And he'd been in the world long enough to know that how a person acted counted for more than what church they attended.

Rose might have been raised Protestant, which made her a heretic, by his family's measure. But she was as good a woman as any he'd met. Gentle. Kind. Generous. Sweet. Pure, too.

As he walked back to his hotel, he resolved to inspect this young man of Campbell's at the Grand Ball. If he is a good man, well and good. But the kind of man Campbell was likely to support? Well, Rose should have a choice. That was all. She should be able to choose. Perhaps he could offer her a job in one of his stores? She could not be worse off than she was as Campbell's unpaid skivvy.

Five

"And you are to do as Mr Hackerton tells you, Laura," Uncle Campbell said. "You are not to dance unless he says you might. Do not drink the punch, for I do not trust those Freemasons not to put ruinous liquor into it. And you are not to dance with Thomas O'Bryan, do you hear me?"

With her uncle's admonitions ringing in her ears, Rose set off to the dance. Walking on a gentleman's arm was strange. Mr Hackerton was much shorter than Thomas, barely an inch taller than she, and the strange pull she felt when with Thomas simply wasn't there, the one that urged her to tuck herself up against his side. She kept a decorous distance between them.

Conversing with Mr Hackerton was easy enough. She had only to nod, smile, and make meaningless comments at appropriate intervals. "Oh, really?" "Well, I never." "Indeed." "How nice." After a while, she began trotting them out in order, without regard to Mr Hackerton's conversation. He did not notice, continuing to regale her with story after story of his victories over customers, suppliers, employees, and household.

She could not marry this man. She could not. He was no less a bully than Uncle Campbell, and she shuddered to think of putting herself under his thumb. Whatever the marriage bed involved, she was sure she would rather clean floors in a boarding house than submit to such intimacies with Mr Hackerton.

The new Murphy's Assembly Room, on Rattray Street, was transformed with flowers and lights and great, hanging swaths of white and gold fabric. Mr Hackerton showed their tickets at the door, and attempted to hurry her through to the main hall, but Rose hung back. "I need to tidy my hair, Sir," she told him. "I will come to join you directly."

She waited her turn at the small mirror, smoothed the hair that had been disarranged by her bonnet, and spent a few more minutes tidying and arranging her clothes, reluctant to re-join her escort.

But he was not in the entrance foyer when she emerged from the ladies' retiring room. Such a small man; perhaps she was missing him in the crowd? She began to weave between the groups of people who had stopped to greet one another, or who were lined at the door of the main room, waiting to enter. No. No Mr Hackerton.

"Are you on your own, Miss?" A strange man rested a hand on her arm, and she flinched. "Thank you, no," she stammered, backing away. He persisted, following her. "Would you care for a dance, Miss?"

Her backward progress was arrested as she came up against a solid body, and her momentary panic turned to relief at Mr O'Bryan's warm tones. "There you are, Miss Campbell. So easy to get lost when there are so many people." She looked up at him with a warm smile, and the man who had addressed her melted into the crowd.

"Have you become separated from your escort?" Mr O'Bryan asked. "May I find him for you?"

"I thought he was waiting here for me, Mr O'Bryan, but he must have gone on inside. I don't suppose that man meant any harm."

"Probably not," Mr O'Bryan agreed. But his eyes remained wary as he offered her his arm.

How different it was making her way through the shifting masses shielded by Mr O'Bryan's protective arm and cheerful quips. Once they were through the door and in the main room, the crowd opened out enough for her to see Mr Hackerton talking to several other people from the church, and she directed Mr O'Bryan in that direction.

Hackerton saw them coming and abandoned his conversation to bustle in their direction, glowering. "Miss Campbell, what are you about?"

"Mr Hackerton, may I make known to you Mr O'Bryan, the nephew of my Aunt Agnes? Mr O'Bryan was kind enough to escort me through all the people."

"O'Bryan." Mr Hackerton gave a short nod, his frown not a whit abated.

"We have met," Mr O'Bryan told Rose, returning the nod with no more affability than Mr Hackerton. "I commend Miss Campbell to your care, Hackerton. The crowd presses more roughly than a lady likes."

Two dogs circling with their hackles raised, and Rose would not be the bone between them. She murmured her thanks to Mr O'Bryan and left the two gentlemen to their dispute, passing them to greet Mr and Mrs MacTavish and their adult children.

Mr Hackerton followed her a moment later, but by then, she was admiring Miss Minnie MacTavish's gown and Miss Molly MacTavish's fine Indian shawl, and having her own shawl— Thomas's beautiful Christmas gift—admired in turn.

"Virtue is a woman's best adornment," Mr Hackerton proclaimed, offending Mr MacTavish, who complained. "Ye are no' sayin' that me Minnie and Molly are no' virtuous, Hackerton?"

In the interconnected web of Dunedin's merchant world, MacTavish and his carrier business were crucial. Hackerton was quick to deny any such intention, and with luck, would forget Rose's own crimes in the ensuing fuss.

After three country dances—one with Hackerton, one with the oldest MacTavish son, and one she watched from the sidelines— the band began a waltz. Rose would not dance the scandalous dance, of course, though she watched wistfully as the MacTavish girls, one after another, accepted invitations from young men approved by their father.

How lovely the dancers looked. Gentlemen in black tailcoats; merchants and clerks and carters and miners in their Sunday best, turning and circling around the floor to the music, the women in their arms like so many flowers, with their full skirts swaying, especially those whose exaggerated bells were supported by fashionable hoops.

She did not realise she was smiling and humming until Mr Hackerton touched her arm to gain her attention. "You are not listening, Miss Campbell. I said I am surprised at Mr MacTavish, allowing his daughters to participate in such a riotous activity. A country dance, yes. Some consider such levity unbecoming, but I cannot allow that the Lord frowns on all dancing, when we are told David danced. Not the waltz, however."

Rose had a sudden image of the David from the colour plate illustration she had seen at the Athenaeum, that beautiful naked youth with a slingshot over his shoulder. The man who danced before the Ark, but also had several wives at once and pursued Bathsheba even to the point of murder, would have loved the waltz, she thought.

Mr Hackerton droned on, and she listened with half an ear, so her nods and shakes—the only conversational input he required—were not totally inappropriate. The rest of her mind was on the dancing. Had Papa not died in his futile quest for riches, he would have permitted her to waltz. Papa laughed at his brother's rigid ways and enjoyed seeing his daughter in pretty dresses.

The waltz was followed by another country dance, into which Hackerton condescended to lead her. "For you are not to think, Miss Campbell, that I will forbid my wife all frivolity," he told her when they took their turn to stand aside for the other couples. "Though I cannot approve of your acquaintance with that scoundrel, O'Bryan."

"He is my aunt's nephew, Mr Hackerton," she protested, ignoring the reference to a marriage the man had not discussed with her.

"Yes, and it is a great pity," Hackerton shook his head, as if in sorrow. "Mrs Campbell is a good woman, and for her sister to marry a half-breed, and a Papist half-breed, at that! Campbell has told me all about it. Then for that young man to come here with his foreign ways and his foreign goods…"

It was their turn in the dance again, and Rose spent her time in the figures wondering why Mr Hackerton was so upset with Mr O'Bryan.

"What has Mr O'Bryan done, Mr Hackerton?" she ventured, when they stood out again.

"Why, that scoundrel plans on importing his own supplies for his stores in the fields, instead of buying from us here in Dunedin! Are our goods not good enough for him?" Hackerton continued to rave during each break, though Rose rather thought that most of what he said was jealousy.

She sat to watch several more dances, while Hackerton chatted with various business contacts. Mr O'Bryan did not sit out a dance, though he did not dance twice with the same partner.

She was watching him promenade his latest partner up between the couples in a line dance, one hand gracefully on his hip, and the other holding the lady's high between them, when she felt a sharp pinch on her arm.

"Miss Campbell!" Hackerton frowned at her startled yelp. "You will not embarrass me by panting after that whelp."

"Mr Hackerton!" Rose rubbed her arm furiously. How dare he pinch her? And how dare he accuse her of... of inappropriate thoughts about Mr O'Bryan?

"I expect propriety at all times, Miss Campbell, and you will do well to keep that in mind. My wife must be beyond reproach. Beyond reproach, I say."

"I am not your wife, Mr Hackerton. Nor have you asked me to take that role."

Mr Hackerton waved off the objection. "No, that is all organised. Your uncle has agreed. The banns are to be called this Sunday." Sensing, perhaps, that this was not to her liking, he grabbed her hand in one of his pudgy fists and patted it. "You will find me a generous husband, if you are an obedient wife, Laura, my dear."

Suddenly, Rose was furious, being misnamed the last straw. "Mr Hackerton, you are much mistaken if you think I will be your wife, obedient or otherwise. It is my agreement you need, not my uncle's, and I do not give it."

Mr Hackerton smiled indulgently. "There, there. It is all understood. You must trust your uncle to know what is best for you, my dear, Laura."

"I am not called Laura. Nor have I given you permission to be so familiar. Nor shall I."

"Miss Campbell, you forget yourself." Mr Campbell was becoming annoyed. "Campbell has promised me your hand, and we will be wed before the end of the month."

"No, Mr Hackerton," Rose insisted, "we will not."

"Is this man annoying you, Miss Campbell?" Concentrating on her altercation with Hackerton, she had not heard Mr O'Bryan approach.

"This is between me and my betrothed, O'Bryan, and nothing to do with you," Hackerton bellowed.

O'Bryan's eyes shifted to Rose, doubt clouding them.

"He is not my betrothed," Rose said, her voice louder than she intended, and was startled to hear a hiss. Looking around, she realised they were the focus of attention in this corner of the room, and several people from the church congregation were frowning at her.

She shrank towards Mr O'Bryan, and he rose to the occasion. "Will you honour me with a dance, Miss Campbell?"

"You will not." Hackerton, too, had noticed the interest of the bystanders and lowered his voice accordingly. "Miss Campbell, you will not dance with this man. And a waltz, at that!"

Rose ignored him, though her hand trembled on Mr O'Bryan's arm as he led her onto the floor. She would not faint. She would not be ill. She would sail around the room in Mr O'Bryan's arms, and if she were a poor, brown sparrow against the colourful flowers that had sailed there before, she would make the most of her opportunity. She would, for certain, pay the price when her uncle found out, but she would have the pleasure first.

<hr />

Miss Campbell slowly relaxed into the dance, and as she gave herself over to the music and the movement, Thomas let the tension drain out of his own muscles. Still, he kept an eye on Hackerton, until he saw the man push his way to the front door and leave.

Thomas had tried to do business with Hackerton when he first arrived in Dunedin, but soon realised the man was a bully and a coward, and a poor businessman, at that. Thomas had found other suppliers for the local products he couldn't easily ship in. Hackerton had not been pleased.

He hoped Miss Campbell was telling the truth when she said she was not betrothed to Hackerton. The thought of this timid, little mouse in the hands of that brute made him firm his grip, pulling her a little closer, and he was thrilled to his core when she came willingly, trustingly, looking up into his eyes, smiling as he swung her around a turn in the dance, then reluctantly let her out again to the socially acceptable distance.

He could dance with her all night, hold her in his arms for a lifetime, protecting her from any chill wind that shrivelled that sweet trust… He tried to remind himself she was wrong for him—wrong faith, wrong country, wrong in every way. He needed a strong woman who would be an asset in the business, not a shy, wee lassie that needed to be sheltered and cosseted.

Though she was a hard worker, he would give her that. And she stood up to Hackerton, right enough. He chuckled. Hackerton had not expected that. Thomas had thought the man would explode.

Rose, oblivious to his thoughts, chuckled with him. "This is such fun, Mr O'Bryan. Lovely to watch, but even lovelier to do!"

"You've never waltzed before?" He could not believe it. She followed his steps as if they had practiced together half their lives.

But she shook her head, vigorously. "Not in company. My father taught me the steps, but I have never been to a ball before."

"You dance beautifully," he assured her, looking down into her laughing eyes. How lovely she was. And stronger than she knew, with her ability to put the nastiness with Hackerton aside and simply enjoy the moment.

"Will you be in Dunedin long, Mr O'Bryan?"

"I return to the fields tomorrow, Miss Campbell. I need to supervise the store until Mrs Moffat arrives, and then I will move to the new store in Arrow."

He told her his plans for the second store, barely listening to what he was saying, only knowing how good it felt to dance with her, talk to her.

The music was ending. The dance was over, and he had to let her go. He swallowed, abruptly breathless with longing to keep her in his arms forever.

It was difficult to speak past the yearning, but he managed to sound calm as he asked, "What do you wish to do now, Miss Campbell? Is there someone else I can take you to? Do you wish me to stay with you?"

"I am sure the MacTavishes will see me home."

But when Thomas escorted her to the people she pointed out, the younger members of the family turned their backs, and the mother said, "You have chosen this outsider over one of our own, Miss Campbell. Let him see you home. If, indeed, you dare to return to your uncle's house, after showing such ingratitude."

Without a word, Miss Campbell turned and walked stiffly away, two high spots of cover on her cheeks, and Thomas, after tossing the woman a scowl that should have shrivelled her where she stood, hurried after her.

Miss Campbell said nothing until they had collected their coats and were walking through the silent streets, their breath condensing into small clouds as they walked. "She lets her own daughters waltz," she burst out. "And she would not marry them to Mr Hackerton, either!"

"Is your uncle…? Will your uncle make you marry?" He would marry her himself, rather than leave her to that fate—a solution that seemed sweeter to him the more he thought about it.

"He cannot. This is the nineteenth century. A woman cannot be married against her will."

She sounded very firm, but wills can be suborned. He pulled her into the recess of a shop doorway, so they could continue the discussion out of the wind.

"Will he be cross, Miss Campbell? Should I talk to him?"

She shook her head, decisively. "That would make it worse, I do not doubt, though it is kind of you to offer. But what can he do, Mr O'Bryan? Shut me in my room to think over my sins, beyond a doubt, but he will let me out when there are chores to be done."

She believed in her own safety. Looking into her eyes in the half-light, he could see the certainty there. Without conscious thought, he laid his hand gently along the side of her face, stroking her cheek with his thumb.

"If you have any doubt, Rose, and think Campbell might hurt you, or do something else to force you to his will, you do not have to go back."

She opened her mouth, already shaking her head, and he hurried on to say his piece before she could object. "You could marry me. I don't flatter myself that I am a prize, but I am a better bet than Hackerton. Marry me, and let me care for you, Rose." He bent, curving low to capture her mouth. It was as soft and full as it looked though, at first, stiff and unresponsive.

But she followed his lead in this as she had in the dance, and what had begun as an impulsive gesture to prevent her from saying no became a luxurious vortex that spun him out of space and time until he was oblivious of everything except the giving, the taking, the sharing of their lips, their tongues, their mouths.

She looked dazed when he drew back. Well, good. *He* was dazed. He gathered her against his chest and rested his cheek on her hair. "Marry me, Rose," he repeated.

"I cannot, Thomas. You will be gone tomorrow. And we barely know one another."

"You could travel with one of the families, and we could be married when we arrive at the fields. I know we haven't known one another long, but I know you are brave and true. I know you feel like Heaven in my arms. I know I can talk to you for hours about anything under the sun."

"Oh, Thomas… I wish…" She gathered herself, pulling away a little, so she could look up at him. He took heart that she stayed within his arms.

"If you are still of the same mind next time you come to Dunedin, Thomas, I would be proud to be your wife." She blushed, casting her eyelashes down onto her cheeks. "Proud," she repeated.

Later, locked in her room, lying, bruised and bleeding, on her bed, after the worst beating her uncle had ever given her, she regretted that choice. She should have gone with him, in her Sunday best, leaving behind her meagre belongings. But would he have taken her? And wouldn't he have regretted it?

Aunt Agnes had screamed at her, but Uncle Campbell had been silent in his fury. Mr Hackerton, who had been at the house when she arrived home, had declared himself released from his contract by her outrageous behaviour. So, one good thing had come from all the fuss.

Even days later after she was able to drag herself from her bed, she was not permitted to leave the house. Instead, the new maid was sent on errands, and Rose was set to scouring the floors and emptying the chamber pots.

She endured. Surely they would not keep her prisoner forever? Indeed, after the third time the servant came home with no change, having overspent on meat and vegetables that were old and tired, and resigned from her post when scolded, Rose was once more sent out to press every coin until it squeaked, though her time was closely monitored, so she dared add nothing to the errand on which she was sent.

Thomas would return for her, as he had promised. Or, she would find a position and make her own way.

While she waited, life fell back into a normal pattern, except that members of the congregation turned their backs to her when they saw her on the street, or even in church. It was not important. She had only to endure until she finished healing, or until Thomas returned.

Mr Hackerton came first.

Six

"He is prepared to take you despite your behaviour," Aunt Agnes crowed. And Uncle Campbell was gleefully discussing the supply contract the marriage would, apparently, seal.

At first, neither heard Rose's quiet "No."

Aunt Agnes was the first to notice. "No? What do you mean, 'No'?"

"No, Aunt Agnes. I will not marry Mr Hackerton. I would not marry Mr Hackerton, even if I had not promised to wait for Mr O'Bryan."

The storm broke, as she had expected, and she bowed her head and ignored them both. They could lock her up, beat her, starve her, but they could not force her to marry against her will.

"…And you need not think I'll continue to house such an ungrateful Jezebel. You disgraceful harlot, consorting with the Whore of Babylon. I'll not have it, I tell you. Obey me or leave my house, Laura Rose Campbell."

"Very well, Uncle. I will leave."

Rose was nearly as surprised as her uncle to hear the words coming from her mouth.

She packed her few bits and pieces while Aunt Agnes watched to make sure she took nothing that wasn't hers. In silence, her aunt by marriage escorted her down the stairs and out the front door.

When Rose was out on the public walk, Aunt Agnes looked over her shoulder, a quick, furtive glance back into the house. "Wait there, girl. Just for a moment." She disappeared back into the house and was back in moments.

"You have been a good girl, Laura, on the whole. I will miss you. Here." She pressed something into Rose's hand: a purse, with a few shifting lumps that must be coins. "Thomas is a good boy, for all he is a Papist. He has written to you. Campbell made me read the letters and burn them. He will make an honest woman of you." A quick, awkward hug, and a brush of papery lips on Rose's cheek, and she was gone, the front door closed between them.

Rose raised her empty hand to her cheek in wonder. Who knew Aunt Agnes had a heart? She had never shown any signs of it before.

The front door flew open again, and Rose was just in time to hide the purse in the folds of her skirt, before her uncle was screaming in her face.

"Go then, if you are going. Don't litter my doorstep, you foul tramp!" He caught her a buffet that knocked her into the road.

Perhaps he would have hit her again, but a man passing in the street stopped to ask, "Are you all right, Miss?"

"Thank you. I am just leaving." Rose picked up her bag and walked away without a backward look, her heart rising with every step. Thomas had written. Thomas still wanted her. And even if he didn't, surely she could find work, respectable work with a wage and roof over her head?

Right this minute, she knew exactly what to do. At the O'Bryan warehouse, she asked for directions to Mrs Moffat's house. She only hoped the woman had not yet left for the gold fields.

⚬⚬⚬

Thomas stood in the door of his store, admiring the bustle as the crowds passed. This late in the day, many of the area's hopeful, would-be millionaires were coming into town to while away their evening, but they were mostly a cheerful lot. Some would drink every grain of gold dust they'd found, and there would be fights and loud singing, but the New Zealand gold fields enforced a strong ban on guns, so most injuries would be minor.

Soon, Mrs Moffat would arrive, and then, after another week to make sure his new manager could keep the store as well as Thomas did, he could return to Dunedin for Rose. The bonnet trim he had purchased the day after that December shopping expedition sat on the table in his bedchamber, a constant reminder of all the gifts with which he wanted to shower her.

He had wondered, even as he proposed, if her charm would fade with separation. Instead, he wanted her more every day, dreamed of seeing her bright smile over breakfast, imagined her reaction every time he heard a funny conversation or an interesting fact, fantasised about holding her again in his arms, and feeling her burrow trustingly close.

Perhaps, though, she had changed her mind? She had not replied to his letters, sent faithfully on every mail coach. But the Campbells, that poisonous old pair, would not let her reply, he supposed. He held on to that belief, and would, in any case, test it by calling on her. Soon. He could leave soon.

A burst of noise and movement at the other end of the street caught his attention. A wagon train coming into town, full of eager miners and, he hoped, his new shop manager.

There she was, a child on either side, driving a cart laden high with what he assumed were the goods he'd ordered up from the wharves. The others must be walking and, sure enough, at least three children flanked the cart, including one hand in hand with… he caught his breath. Surely, it couldn't be Rose?

But he would know her anywhere, and his legs had not waited for his brain to catch up, but were already carrying him down the street at a stride, and then at a run.

Rose, his Rose, dropped the child's hand and pushed her towards one of the older girls with a quick word, then started towards Thomas, her dear face shining with welcome.

In a moment, he had her in his arms, oblivious to the laughing, cheering crowd of bystanders.

"You came," he said.

"Thomas."

A swollen, ugly, fading bruise disfigured one eye, but she was still the most beautiful sight he had ever seen. He brushed it tenderly with the back of his fingers, before cupping her cheek.

"Marry me, Rose," he asked again.

Her smile answered him before her shy words. "Yes, please, Thomas."

THE END

Kidnapped to Freedom

Stolen from the Georgian plantation just ahead of being sold down the river, Phoebe faces the high seas to be reunited with her brother and sister, and the master's son she once loved. Why then, are her dreams filled with the handsome, masked pirate who captains her rescue ship? (Short story)

Phoebe hurried from shadow to shadow behind the row of cabins. The full moon had risen. She was late. Why did Massa Paddy have to send for her tonight, of all nights! He was drunk, which was no surprise, for he'd been drunk since the Master died. The drink, though, had left him limp, for which he blamed her, until the punishment he administered excited him enough to finish.

Then he'd collapsed on top of her, and it had taken time to edge out from beneath his weight.

Beneath the constant susurration of the cicadas, she could hear murmurs of conversation inside the cabins. He wouldn't look for her when he woke; he would assume she'd gone back to the cabin she shared with the children.

Had he made her miss her chance? Their chance—for she wouldn't go without the children.

Phoebe felt some of the tension leave her when she saw them waiting for her behind their cabin. Venus balanced little Patricia on her hip, and Joe cradled Baby. Jake ran to meet her, taking her hand for the few steps back to her family.

Now, if only whoever it was had waited. If only it were true and not a trap. Phoebe hoisted one of the bundles she and Venus had hidden here earlier this morning, before the day's exertions had begun.

"Jake, take this bundle, and Venus, give me Pat-a-cake, and take the rest of our things." The three-year-old didn't stir during the transfer, just settled her head into the curve of Phoebe's neck. She slept like a rock, that girl, just like Massa Paddy, who'd sired her.

She led her little flock down the path into the woods. She was putting a lot of trust in the letter the peddler had slipped to her three weeks ago. But what choice did she have? Miz Nettie was going to sell them to the slave trader—Phoebe and all the five children left to her.

When she'd first made the threat, Phoebe had hoped it was just the sorrow speaking. Miz Nettie had been wild with grief since her husband, Mist' Chan, fell from his horse and died, followed in short order by Ol' Massa Blake, his father, who took apoplexy when her husband turned up dead.

At least, Miz Nettie had been wild since the will was read.

But she meant her threat. Massa Paddy said the trader was coming this way next week. He was sorry, he said, because he was fond of Phoebe, but her sewing skills meant she would fetch a high price and find a good place, so she wasn't to worry.

Not to worry? Not to worry about her children being taken from her and sold away, probably down the river? Venus, at nearly twelve, was old enough and pretty enough to catch a master's eye, and Joe already did a man's job in the fields, but at least here, Massa Paddy had a reason to treat him fair, as long as she accommodated his needs.

Please, God, let the letter be true, please, God. It had been her constant prayer these last weeks. Please, God, it was from her brother, as it seemed to be. It would read like nonsense to anyone else opening it, but she knew.

"To the gentle Lady of the Lake. Sir Morien bids you, on the night of the first full moon after the natal day of the loathsome Sir Kay, to go to the place where the Parfait Knight shared his tales of chivalry, and from thence, to seek the Holy Grail."

She read, but not well. She couldn't ask for help, but she managed to puzzle most of it out. The names she'd seen before, long ago when she learned to read. What was 'natal day'? She fretted over that one for a week, until she overheard a visiting preacher comment how sad it was that the Master had died on his natal day.

Sir Morien—the name Mist' Phineas had given her brother, Cudjo, in the long sagas they had played out at his direction in these very woods. Mist' Finn was the Parfait Knight, of course, and they readily agreed to refer to his older brother, Mist' Chauncey, as Sir Kay. The Holy Grail, to them all, was freedom.

This was her third note in the twelve years since Mist' Finn had run away, taking her younger sister and brother with him. The first, some eighteen months after they had left, was just five words. 'We found Avalon. All safe.' The second, five years ago, had offered escape 'at the abode of the Lady of the Lake.' The little harbour where Mist' Finn had kept his sailboat might as well have been on the moon, for all the chance she had of reaching it that particular week.

But this time, the meeting point was right here on the plantation.

They were heading for the Woods House, behind which, in stolen moments, Mist' Finn had taught the three of them to read, using the books about the Arthurian legends he so loved.

Please, God, she was not too late. Please, God, it was not a trap.

Val waited in the shadow of the trees. It must be at least thirty minutes past moonrise. She wasn't coming. Again. Five years ago, he had waited the whole night and come back again the next. This time, if he couldn't carry Phoebe off tonight, he'd have to give up. It had taken all his powers of persuasion to convince his crew to make one try. They weren't privateers. The letters of marque that let them take an American ship while the United States and England were at war wouldn't cover a land raid on a plantation. If she didn't come now, the men wouldn't agree to a second attempt.

There! Someone was coming. He straightened in anticipation. Yes, it was her—twelve years older and a mature women, rather than the girl he remembered, but even in the moonlight, he couldn't mistake her.

She wasn't alone. He couldn't take a herd of children with him! What was she thinking?

He stepped out from the sheltering trees. The mask would hide his face, and his voice had never been the same since the last time he had been close enough to Phoebe to speak, when Chan tried to strangle him for the presumption.

"Are you Phoebe?" He was twelve years older, too, and a man changed more from seventeen to twenty-nine than a woman did, but he couldn't risk being seen and recognised by anyone on the plantation.

She nodded. He noted that she gathered the children protectively behind her, but the older boy, his face grimly intent, evaded the sweep of her arm and stepped in front. Brave little bantam rooster.

"I was commissioned to take one woman to her brother in Canada, not a passel of brats," he said.

"Can't leave without ma babies, Sir." Her voice was barely a whisper, but determined.

Her children? All of them? His brother's children, then, possibly. Probably. He surveyed them quickly. Yes, the little bantam had the Blake look, and the girl rocking the baby could be a darker version of the childhood portrait of his mother that hung in the parlour.

The men wouldn't like it, but he was taking them all, and be damned.

He met the eyes of each in turn as he said, "You must be quiet. Not a sound. Do everything I say, and I will take you to your uncle in Canada."

"Perry, give the signal." He gave the command over his shoulder, not waiting to see if it was obeyed. Perry could be trusted to carry out the raid with maximum noise and minimum damage. He didn't want anyone actually killed, but he did hope many slaves would take the chance to escape in the confusion, masking the disappearance of one maid and her children.

He led the way down to the creek, where Jimson stood ready to row them back out to the coast and the waiting ship.

Phoebe startled awake at the knock on the door. Three of the children still slept on the bed in the small, but luxurious, room. No. Mist' Finn had called it a cabin. Venus and Jake were awake, but unmoving, in the tangle of little bodies, watching her with anxious eyes. She smiled to reassure them and wished she had someone to reassure her.

Another knock.

When she opened it, the little man who had shown them to this cabin nodded at her. "The cap'n wants to see ye, Ma'am."

He'd called her 'Ma'am' last night, too. Unaccountably, being addressed so courteously made her even more nervous, as if an overseer hid just out of sight, waiting to punish her for aping a lady.

"Do I come with you?" she asked.

"He'll come to ye, Ma'am. In a few minutes, like. To have breakfast with ye and the nippers. He thought ye might want to have a wash first." The man handed her the jug he was holding, filled with steaming hot water, and crossed the cabin to place the towels draped on his arm across the back of a chair.

He turned in time to save the jug as the ship lurched, and she lost her balance.

"Ye'll get yer sea legs soon, Ma'am," he said, not unkindly, and put the jug into a hole obviously made for it, next to a basin in a hole of its own.

She and the children were washed and tidied before another knock heralded the man from last night. He was still masked, his eyes glittering at her, his chin and mouth showing, but the rest of his face covered in black cloth.

The little man scurried in behind him, carrying a laden tray that smelled of bacon.

Venus, who had been looking a little ill, gave a piteous moan. Before Phoebe could react, the masked man, moving with blinding speed, had grabbed the jug, now emptied of wash water, and placed it under Venus' chin. He was just in time, and Jake was the next to say, "Phoebe, I don't feel too good."

Phoebe hurried to feel his forehead. What could be wrong with them? They were never sick!

Some of her fear must have conveyed itself to the masked man, because he said, calmly, "Seasickness, Miss Blake. They will recover once they are used to the motion of the boat.

"Jenkins, remove the bacon, will you? Miss Blake and I will have breakfast in the wardroom with whichever of the children is well enough to join us."

He was holding the jug with one hand and calmly supporting the vomiting girl with the other. "Oh, and Jenkins, bring some buckets, please? I rather think this young lady may have imitators."

This was not how Val had imagined their reunion; him with a bucket under the chin of one of the children Phoebe had borne his brother, while she tended to another child who, by the look of him, had a different father. He shuddered to think what her life had been like.

If he'd stayed, could he have protected her? He had asked himself the question many times. At seventeen, he'd been half-inclined to blame Phoebe for being selected by his brother. His jealousy had made it easier for him to agree to run with the others after Chan had caught them together and then refused to let Phoebe out of his sight.

The more Val mixed with the freedmen of colour in the Maritime States, the more he realised how arrogant and stupid he had been. And after he'd rescued Perry from some privateers and heard his anguish at some of the things his sister had been through, he'd felt even worse. He and Perry made a raid on the Georgia plantation that held Perry's sister and won her free, and Val had been planning to do the same for Phoebe ever since.

Phoebe had never encouraged Chan. And he'd known that then.

Reassured that seasickness was natural, and the children weren't dying, Phoebe was saying something: apologising for her children being sick, promising to clean up after them, trying to take the jug so she could tend to both children at once. Did she think he would beat her because the ship's lurching disturbed their stomachs? Yes, in her experience, that was probably normal behaviour for a white man.

"No need to apologise, Ma'am," he said, as gently as he could. "It takes most people a while to catch their sea legs. Some experienced sailors are sick for the first days of every trip."

Jenkins brought more water and buckets. "They'll be better on deck, Cap'n," he suggested. "I could set a hammock for 'em, out o' the way, like?"

Val had hoped to keep Phoebe from the crew's sight. She was lovely, and they were men. But, he reminded himself, they were men he trusted, for the most part.

"See it done, Jenkins. Ma'am, once the children are settled, you and I need to have a talk."

The oldest boy, the smaller girl, and the baby joined them for breakfast, while Jenkins sat with the middle boy and the older girl. Both the afflicted looked better for being out in the fresh air, though it was too early to challenge their stomachs with food.

Phoebe looked uncertainly at the table.

"Serve the children," Val suggested, "then you and I will serve ourselves. Shall we try them on porridge? It is a bit like grits, but made from oats."

The children found porridge very much to their liking. The oldest boy, who Phoebe called Joe, spooned porridge into the baby, and the littlest girl fed herself.

Val filled a plate for Phoebe, who looked surprised when he gave it to her.

"Where I come from, gentlemen serve ladies," he told her.

"I ain't... I am not a lady. I am just a seamstress. A slave and a seamstress."

"Not a slave now. Not anymore," Val said. "And not just a seamstress, either. You are the older sister of Joseph and Benita Copeland, proprietors of one of the finest hotels in St John's, Toronto, a free woman, and a lady of considerable wealth in your own right, Miss Blake."

Phoebe shook her head, a sharp negation. "Not 'Blake.'"

She clapped her hand over her mouth, as if to catch the words, then dropped it again and straightened her back. "You say I am free and wealthy. Then I will not bear that man's name. Let his widow keep it."

Val admired her clear diction. She had always had a facility with languages and could speak English as good as his, but he was fascinated by how quickly she dropped the slave patois. It took a few moments for him to process what she'd actually said. "Widow? Chauncey Blake is dead?"

"Yes. You knew him?"

She was quick. Now Val should tell her who he was. But the same impulse that led him to retain the mask ruled him still. "I did," he said, "to my sorrow."

Had their father not intervened, Chan would probably have killed Val twelve years ago. Twenty-four years to seventeen is not a fair match. Val's last memory of his brother was of his face twisted in anger and hatred, as he struggled against the restraining arms of the overseers to come back and beat Val some more.

There had been no word of Chan's death from Val's friends in Charleston. Mind you, since they found themselves on opposite sides in the war, the correspondence had been sporadic, at best.

"When did he die?"

"Three weeks ago. He was thrown by his horse and broke his neck."

"There'll not be many who will grieve, I imagine," Val said. "His wife, his father. Maybe some of his friends."

"Miz Blake, she be happy to be a widow, I think, except Ol' Massa Blake lived just a week longer than his son, so she loses everything but her widow's portion. She's mad enough to spit. She'll be still madder when she finds us gone. She thought to get a good price for us from the traders."

It was a lot to take in. His brother dead. His father dead. His sister-in-law disinherited, and planning to sell Phoebe—and who else?

"Who inherits?" Val asked. Chan and Nettie had no children, he knew, but his father had a low opinion of most of the Blake cousins.

"Phineas Blake," Phoebe said. "Mist' Chan's younger brother. He's been gone a long time, but Ol' Massa Blake, he never changed his will."

Over the next few days, Phoebe found herself telling the captain a little about her life. He sought her out when she was on deck, insisted that she and the older children take their meals with him and his officers, invited her to walk with him in the evening.

At her request, he called her Mrs Morien and assured her that her brother and sister would be waiting to welcome her home. Beneda—she called herself Benita now—was a widow with a child, "though not likely to remain single for long, Joseph says. A number of men have expressed an interest."

Joseph was the name Cudjo now used. He was, Captain Val said, enjoying the life of a highly eligible bachelor too much to settle down, much to the despair of the local ladies and the exasperation of his sister.

To Phoebe, the stories seemed like the legends Mist' Finn had told her long ago—she could not comprehend the life her sister and brother led. Cautiously at first, and then greedily when he laughed and complied, she asked for more and more details, more and more tales about this strange, new life to which Captain Val would deliver her.

Venus and Jake were soon over their illness. Phoebe had little to do, apart from keeping the younger three entertained and out from under the feet of the crew, helped by the two older children. The trip was a holiday such as they had never known. All but the youngest were used to working until they dropped. For an overseer, Paddy O'Keefe had been indulgent to the children of his reluctant mistress, even giving his daughter his name. But they had to work as hard as any of the others, and he would not have lifted a finger to save even his own get from the traders.

Not like Finn. Finn had taken a beating for her, had stolen her brother and sister away to save them when Ol' Massa Blake had decided to sell them. Joe was Mast' Chan's get, and Patsy and Baby were O'Keefe's. Jake and his sister, dear, lost Mina, were bred on her by another slave, at Ol' Massa Blake's command. Quaco, or Jacob, as the white owners called him, had been a kind and gentle man, and she'd been fond of him. But Finn was the one she dreamt of, the one she thought of when she woke in the night.

She hoped that Venus was Finn's daughter, made in that one week they'd had before Mast' Chan had found them together. She'd taken a beating for that, and so had Finn. But Mast' Chan couldn't take the memories from her.

Finn, his head full of knights and chivalry, hadn't wanted to bed her. But Mast' Chan had already announced his intention to have her when he got back from a trip to Charleston, and she wanted her first time to be with someone who would be kind. That's what she'd told him: someone who would be kind. She didn't tell him that she loved him. She knew better than that.

And he was kind, too, though the first time had been awkward and clumsy. Two virgins together, they had to work out how things fitted. She'd giggled, she remembered, and he chuckled, too, but the smile froze on his face as he entered her, and the discomfort he caused was nothing compared to the dawning wonder on his face.

She was thinking about Finn one evening, about a week into their journey, taking out her memories, one by one, to examine them and gloat over them and tuck them safely away again. The older children had wandered off to the kitchen, where the cook always welcomed them, avowing his intention to put some beef on their bones before the ship arrived in Halifax. The little children were settled in the cabin—the captain's cabin, she realised now. Captain Val was sharing with the first mate, a man of colour he called Perry, who he treated as an equal and a friend.

She was thinking of Finn, not the captain. Not of how he helped her up a ladder earlier in the day, and his hand had lingered for a moment on her hip; not of the way his eyes followed her whenever she was on deck. If she were honest with herself, she knew he watched her, because her eyes sought his every time she came on deck. Why did memories of Finn's boyish face turn, unaccountably, into Captain Val's masked face, with the firm, square angles of his cheek and chin, and the amused quirk that seemed to always linger in one corner of his mouth?

The first mate's roar startled her, and she whipped around, cringing and protecting her head with her arm. But his anger was for a sailor who had abandoned a rope without properly coiling it, and he passed Phoebe without a glance to explain to the sailor, in precise, incisive terms, what could happen if the rope tangled when it was needed, and how long the sailor would spend mending sails in penance, so he would never forget again.

Phoebe, who had expected a careless blow, if not an outright beating, felt something uncurl inside her, a soft, tentative tendril of… what? Hope? Comfort? A sense of safety?

Too early for the last. The captain had warned her that American privateers or the American navy might stop the ship at any time until they made port in Canada. But here, yes, here on this ship, she felt safe.

The sailor made excuses and apologies as he recoiled the rope correctly.

"I were that tired, Mister Peregrine, and it were near the end of my deck time, and then Mickey saw fins off the bow, and I went to see. I meant to come back, Mister Peregrine, honest. It won't happen again, Sir, that it won't."

Peregrine? That was the name of one of the black knights in Finn's Arthurian Tales—Sir Morien, Sir Peregrine. Others, too. What a fitting name for a man of colour.

She said that to the mate as he passed on the way back to his watching post.

"Peregrine was the name of one of the knights from Africa in the stories of King Arthur."

"Yes," the mate replied, "that's what Val said when he gave it to me. He fair loves those stories, Mrs Morien."

A polite nod was the only response she could manage. Her mind was racing. Val. Short for Percival? Percival was the perfect knight, the Parfait Knight of the tales, the role Finn had sought with all the poetry in his soul.

As she crossed back to the rail, adding up all the little clues she'd noticed this past week without being aware of them, he came from below and made a straight line for her.

"Good evening, Mrs Morien." The slight husk in his voice had been turning her knees to water all week. Quickly, before her fears choked the words in her throat, she said, "Finn, when are you going to take off the mask?"

The captain went completely still. Then, slowly, he raised his hands to the back of his head, fumbled with the strings of the mask, and let it fall into one hand.

A man changes a great deal between seventeen and twenty-nine. She knew him, though. She should have known him a week ago, by his eyes alone. She clamped firmly down on the hurt, that he'd felt the need to hide from her. He owed her nothing. She owed him everything. He had saved her brother and sister. He was in the process of saving her and her children. He clearly wanted not to acknowledge her, and he had every right.

"You do not need to wear the mask," she told him. "I understand. I have no claim on you, and I will not be a nuisance." She made to pass him, but he put out a hand to stop her.

"No, Mrs Moriel… Phoebe. No, that isn't it at all. I was… The Blakes have done so much wrong to you, to your family. You must hate us all, especially me. I don't blame you. I left you in that place. I knew what Chan was like, and I walked away. I wore the mask to make you more comfortable. No. That isn't true. I just didn't want to see your eyes when you rejected me. You stay here. Enjoy the fine evening for a while longer. I'll go."

She was so stunned that he was halfway to the hatch before she found her voice, hurrying after him with her hand out. "I don't hate you, Finn. I don't blame you."

He turned, but wouldn't meet her eyes. "I blame myself."

"For what? For trying to protect me and being half killed for it? For saving my brother and my sister, no matter the risk to your own escape? For coming back for me?"

"I came before. The first time, I couldn't get onto the plantation. They had men out with dogs. The second time, we sent you a message, and I waited on the beach, but you didn't come."

"I had the message."

"You couldn't get away, I imagine."

Phoebe shook her head. Mrs Blake had miscarried a child and, in her anger, had her husband's mistress beaten so badly Phoebe had lost the baby she was carrying. It was after that, Phoebe had been sent to Quaco.

Finn—no, Val—Val saw the shadows in her eyes.

"It is over now. You are a free woman and a wealthy one. You never again need to do anything you do not wish." He turned to lean on the rail, looking down at the water folding back from the racing hull.

Phoebe leaned beside him, content to be silent.

After a while, Val spoke. "Phoebe, I know it's too soon. I don't want to press you. I won't press you. You need time to get your family settled, to learn what it is to be free and respected and loved. I want to give you that time. But may I write to you? May I visit from time to time?"

Was he asking what she thought he was asking?

"Yes," she answered briefly, and he turned to her with a smile that lit his whole face.

"I have never forgotten you, Phoebe."

She smiled back, ready to tell him she had never forgotten him, but Mr Perry called him to come and see something on the horizon, outlined by the setting sun, and he left her standing at the rail, watching the water.

Val was right. It was too soon. She needed to get to know her brother and sister again. She needed to get her children started in this life as free people.

But in her heart, the tendril of hope threw off a couple of new leaves, and set down a strong root into the memories of the boy who had once been her champion.

THE END

The Prisoners of Wyvern Castle

Rupert has been imprisoned by his wicked sister, and compelled to wed. His new wife, Madeline, has likewise been threatened into saying her vows. Forced into marriage, they find love, but can they find freedom before it is too late? *The Prisoners of Wyvern Castle* is a prequel to *Embracing Prudence*, due for publication in 2016.

First movement: Allegro furioso

One

As soon as he said the last words of the blessing, the fat priest stepped toward them, a broad smile on his face. "May I be the first to congratulate you, my lord and my lady?"

The man to whom Madeline had just been joined ignored the outstretched hands and whirled around to advance on Lady Wyvern, who stood as he approached.

"Very well. I have done what you demanded. Where is she?"

"Penworth, your manners," Lady Wyvern scolded, but the Earl of Penworth ignored her tone and spoke over the rest of her complaint.

"You promised to return her if I married Graviton's sister. We are wed. I want her back, Lady Wyvern, and I want her now."

Madeline was trying to make sense of it all. The earl had been forced to this marriage as well? By a threat? But to whom? Surely not… not his mistress?

She stole a look at her half-brother, Sir James Graviton, who was openly amused. "Send the boy back to his rooms, Louisa, and my sister with him. His treasure is there, is it not? Oh, do not fret, vicar. You will get your fee and your portion of the wedding breakfast."

The earl fastened on the bit of news about his treasure. "My lady is in the tower?" He headed for the door, but walked straight into the chair in which Lady Wyvern had been sitting, sending it careening across the stone floor, and himself stumbling, arms outstretched to catch himself, until he tripped over another chair and fell heavily.

"Wait until someone can lead you, fool," Lady Wyvern said, impatiently.

Graviton laughed out loud. "Mad, see to your husband," he advised. Madeline ignored the hated nickname, but obeyed the command, kneeling beside the young man stretched out on the floor.

"Are you hurt, my lord?"

"Winded, a little." The earl frowned, a drawing together of heavy brows over his clear, pale eyes. The frown didn't detract from the youthfulness of his face. She was no judge, but she thought him her own age, perhaps younger. She stood and offered her hand to help him rise, but he looked straight past her, as if she were not there.

Graviton was chortling again. "You did not tell her, did you?" Lady Wyvern asked.

"And spoil the joke?" Graviton replied.

Madeline ignored them. "Can I help you up, my lord?"

The earl held out his hand, and Madeline reached for it. Even through her gloves and his, she could feel the strength in his hand, and he made no allowance for the difference in their sizes, so she had to lean back against the weight of him as he pulled himself up. He was tall, this new husband of hers, who couldn't wait to abandon her at the altar. Tall, lean, and handsome. But very young.

"Thank you, Miss, ah, Countess. What is your name again? I am sorry. I was not listening."

Madeline had been listening. He was Rupert Frederick George Arthur John Fleming, 7th Earl of Penworth and Viscount Clearwater.

"Madeline," said Graviton, helpfully. "The family calls her Mad."

Graviton called her Mad. Papa had called her Linnie, and she had been Miss Graviton to the rest of the world. No more. Mother was dead and Miss Graviton was gone, too, wiped out by a few words and her signature on the marriage register.

"Madeline," the earl said, and smiled. It was a kind smile, but still he did not look at her.

"Enough entertainment." Lady Wyvern strode to the door and opened it. "See them to the tower," she commanded the waiting servants. "Penworth, you will find your 'lady' unharmed. But you will do your duty or suffer the consequences."

She swept from the room, the priest on her heels and a grinning Graviton sauntering behind.

The servant who came into the room took the earl by the arm. "This way, my lord." He began to lead the young nobleman towards the door, saying over his shoulder to Madeline, "If you will just follow, my lady, I will show you the way."

Two footmen fell in behind as the servant escorted the earl along the hall. "We're coming to the first corner, my lord," he said, and then, "and in a few steps we'll be on that little flight of stairs."

At the steps, the earl felt ahead with his foot, then mounted the stairs confidently as the footman counted, "one and two and three and four. And now, a straight walk to the next turn, my lord."

All of a sudden, Madeline realised why the earl had not looked at her. Curse Graviton. How was it funny not to tell her the man to whom she had been wed was blind?

The woman he had married——Madeline——had a gentle voice and soft hands. He could tell that much. And she was frightened of her brother, his hated sister's hated lover. That was in her favour, though, of course, it did not mean she could be trusted. She might fear Graviton and still serve him and Lady Wyvern.

Well, it was done now. If she were a snake, he was taking her to his bosom. To his bed, anyway. Lady Wyvern had made it clear that his lady would be chopped into kindling if he didn't attempt to get his new wife with child. Rupert briefly wondered what pressure had been brought to bear on Madeline. He could ask her. Perhaps she would tell the truth. Would he know if she didn't? Rupert shrugged. It did not matter. All that mattered was his lady.

They were climbing the stairs into the tower now. Twenty steps on each flight, two flights to the locked door that gave onto the suite he'd been locked in since he and his sister had first arrived at Wyvern Castle, her island home.

"Do you know where they left her?" he asked his escort.

Morris was a Wyvern servant, assigned with the room. Rupert's own servants had been left at Clearwater Court, and those here were Lady Wyvern's creatures, to a man and a maid. Morris was at least respectful and not unkind.

Ahead of them, someone unlocked the door. He heard the clunk as they locked it behind, once they were within. Most of the escort stayed below, but Rupert could hear the soft footfalls of his new wife on the stone steps, smell the fragrance that clung to her. It was the first thing he'd noticed when they met in the church—the smell of a summer garden after rain, a blend of light, floral perfumes that made him wistful for the freedoms of his boyhood.

"Where is she?" he prompted Morris.

"I don't see her here, my lord. Shall I check upstairs for you?"

He could not wait to hold her in his arms, to check that she had not been damaged. Besides, none but he should touch her. "Take me," Rupert commanded.

His tower prison had three levels: the sitting room where they entered, locked off from below and—if his ears did not betray him—well guarded at all times; the bedchamber they were now passing, Madeline still following behind; and the room at the very top—perhaps once another bedchamber or a study or a workroom.

"She is here, Sir," Morris said.

Now, so close to his life's one comfort, he could hear the blood pounding in his ears, his heartbeat thumping, his breath running short, as if the stairs they climbed had been ten times as high. His head knew his sister would not have hurt his treasure, if only because of the hold it gave her, but his heart would not rest easy till he felt for himself she was whole and unharmed.

Morris led him to a table in the corner, away from the place she usually sat. Too close to the fire! His hands shook, making it hard to open the latches on her case.

From far away, he heard Madeline ask Morris a question and Morris answer. He had no attention to spare them as he lifted his lady, ran his hands over her curves and up her long neck, tentatively tested her strings. She was unharmed. Out of tune, but not damaged.

Swiftly, his fingers sure now, he tightened and rosined the bow string and tuned his violin until she sang to him in her clear pure voice, and he could tuck her under his chin and let the music that had been welled up inside him this last lonely week flow out into the everlasting darkness that surrounded him.

A violin. The earl had been forced to marry her to save his violin. Madeline could not make sense of it; he was a man, and more to the point, an earl. Who could make him act against his will? But Madeline remembered his sister's cold eyes and shuddered. If anyone could, it would be Lady Wyvern. Why, just the fact they were here, in Wyvern Castle, the family seat of the Earls of Wyvern, showed the lengths to which the woman would go. What did Lord Wyvern think of his lady entertaining her lover under this roof?

There was a supper in the sitting room downstairs, Morris said, and Morris's own niece waiting to attend the countess in her bedchamber.

"I will wait a while with the earl," Madeline told him, and the man bowed his way from the room.

The earl was talented. Living retired at Graviton Manor, Madeline had not been to the concerts or *musicales* or other *ton* events she read about in *La Belle Assemblée*, but she had heard enough travelling musicians to know a masterly hand when she heard it.

His long, supple fingers on the bow, on the strings, coaxed forth a torrent of sound that filled the room; at first a sobbing lament, a paean of loss and pain, slowly transforming into dawning delight, and then wild joy, that set her foot tapping with the urge to dance.

She had no idea how long she sat there, lost in the music. When Morris returned to light the candles and lamps, she was surprised to realise the whole afternoon had passed, and the only light in the room came from the last rays of the sun lingering on the stones of the western windows.

His task finished, Morris started to speak, but Madeline waved him off, unwilling to break the spell, so he left the room again.

Something, though, must have disturbed the earl, for he let his hands fall with a deep, satisfied sigh. "She is well," he announced. He crossed the room with firm, certain steps, then stood for a moment before an empty table, the violin in one hand, bow in the other.

"Her case?" he demanded. Madeline hurried to bring it to him, laying it open on the table.

He tenderly placed the violin into the waiting velvet-lined recess shaped to fit, and Madeline held the lid for him while he fitted the bow into its place.

"Thank you."

"You are welcome," Madeline responded.

He flashed a quick grin in her general direction, which made him look even younger. "You have been sitting here the whole time, have you not? You must be famished. I am famished. Shall we go and find supper?"

She took the hand he offered and followed his lead to the door, tugging slightly when he veered too close to the frame. He responded with another of those quick grins and let her guide him safely onto the stairs where he skimmed his free hand down the wall until they reached the sitting-room level.

Morris waited for them with a young woman he introduced as his niece, Polly Morris. She was short and wiry like her uncle, but not uncomely, her sturdy gingham gown covered by a white apron, a few strands of dark hair escaping from her neat, white cap to curl around the thin face.

She bobbed a curtsey, colouring a little when she murmured "Miss" in greeting, then corrected it to "my lady."

"She's a good girl, my lady," Morris assured Madeline.

"I am sure she is," Madeline agreed, thinking the woman no longer a girl. Polly was at least Madeline's age of twenty-two. Most of her mind was on her new husband, the earl, who had dropped her hand and was feeling his way forward to the table where supper was laid.

"My wife and I will serve ourselves," he announced, his hands skimming across the table and stopping to explore when they encountered a plate or a bowl. "Morris, you and the maid can wait up in the bedchamber or outside the rooms, as you wish." He took a seat at one of the two chairs pulled up to the table, licking a finger that had explored a bowl of cream, then stood again, abashed. "I beg your pardon, Madeline. I should have waited until you were seated. Please..." He waved, and Madeline sat in the chair Morris held for her.

The earl had his head turned, clearly listening, and when Morris and Polly disappeared around the corner of the steps leading to the bedchamber, he smiled at Madeline again.

"You do not mind, I hope? I thought we should talk without my sister's spies lurking." He shrugged, an oddly elegant movement. "You could be one, of course. Are you? And would you mind preparing something for me to eat while you answer that? Some meat on a slice of bread would be easy. Something I can hold in my hands without giving you an utter disgust of me. I am not tidy with a knife and fork."

The earl's preference had been considered, with slices of bread and meat available.

"I do not mind," Madeline said, and busied her hands while she thought about how to answer the earl's question. Bluntly was best. "I am not your sister's spy or my brother's. But I imagine that is what a spy would say. Here, my lord. Lamb between two slices of bread, and I have spread a preserve on the bread."

"Thank you. You can call me Rupert if you like. I do not think you are a spy. I do not think the Ice Dragon—my sister, I mean—cares that much what I do, as long as I do not try to escape or to kill myself. And the servants can prevent that. But why would you marry me if you are not her creature? Can you tell me that?"

"The world has no shortage of women who want to marry an earl," Madeline retorted. She was not one of them, though. She could imagine nothing worse than living the kind of life that countesses followed, as far as she could tell from the pages of *Ackermann's Repository* and *The London Gazette*. The London she yearned for—museums, libraries, and bookstores—was a far cry from the London such exalted ladies inhabited.

And yet, here she was.

Rupert laughed, a short, unamused bark. "A blind boy earl imprisoned by his sister and her lover? Hardly. If you sought social success, Madam Countess, you face disappointment."

"I sought to stay at home with my books and my work in the parish," Madeline retorted. And if she had occasionally daydreamed about marriage, it was of marriage at her own level in society, after a respectable courtship.

Her new husband echoed her thoughts. "Yet, here you are." He took another bite of his bread, and chewed meditatively.

Madeline busied herself with her own meal: a serving of pie and some sort of ragout. She could understand Rupert's need to know her motives, but she cringed at the thought of explaining exactly what her brother used to compel her. Perhaps it would be enough just to hint. "Graviton threatened me."

"He threatened me, too. He and the Ice Dragon said they would chop my lady into pieces—my violin, that I inherited from my mother—if I made a fuss or refused to say the vows. What have they taken off you? I will ask for it back. They usually let me have what I ask for. As I said. She just does not much care."

Madeline blushed. "I have it yet. But Graviton said it would be taken from me by force if I did not marry…."

Rupert frowned. "What is it? Do you have it with you? Shall we hide it to keep it safe?"

Madeline could feel the blush spreading all over her body. "I… that is, it is not that kind of a…"

Rupert looked bewildered, and well he might. She was going to have to tell him. "Graviton said he would give me to his friends to… well, to use. Without benefit of clergy. He said I would fetch a tidy sum because…" her voice trailed off.

Rupert took another mouthful of his bread and meat to hide his confusion.

To use how? For what? Whatever Graviton had in mind, it clearly upset Madeline a great deal to speak of it.

"You play very well." His new wife was changing the subject. "I do not think I have ever met a gentleman who played the violin."

"My mother taught me," Rupert said. "She did not think it an unsuitable hobby for an earl." Lady Wyvern disagreed with her stepmother on that point, and had not hesitated to make her opinion heard, but her lord overruled her. Lord Wyvern had said, "Let the boy have his fiddle. God knows, his blindness will bar him from most respectable pursuits."

Lord Wyvern. Where was he, and what role had he played in this marriage his wife had brokered?

Madeline snorted. "Surely an earl may have any hobby he wishes?"

"Yes, so Lord Wyvern says. Madeline, was Lord Wyvern… have you seen Lord Wyvern? At our wedding or at any time since you came to the castle?"

"No, indeed, and I wondered at it! Does he not care what she does? Your sister is Graviton's..." Madeline's voice trailed off.

"She is your brother's lover. They hid it in front of Lord Wyvern, but they have been lovers this last three years." Rupert frowned. "Lord Wyvern is my guardian until I reach my majority next year. I am worried about him, Madeline. Last time I saw him, he said he would return in a sennight, and that was six months past."

"Have you asked the servants? They usually know everything."

"Not at Clearwater. No one there knew of anything untoward. The steward said Lord Wyvern wrote of a delay in London, but that was months ago. He has never gone even a month without visiting me, Madeline, and he always writes when he is away. I asked and asked, but they told me no letters have arrived."

It was an odd break in an established habit, and Madeline sounded as puzzled as Rupert when she asked. "Clearwater is one of Lord Wyvern's estates?"

"One of mine. Ours now, I suppose. The earldom's. My sister and Graviton came to fetch me there a month ago and brought me here. I should have refused to leave Clearwater. My own servants would have protected me, I expect. But they said Lord Wyvern had sent for me, and so I came. And here, the servants obey Louisa, not me."

"And not Lord Wyvern," Madeline stated, rather than asked.

"They will not speak of Lord Wyvern."

There was a second stack of bread and meat on his plate, waiting for his questing hand. Rupert murmured his thanks and took a hearty bite. "Are you eating, Madeline?" He could not hear her moving.

"I... I am not hungry, my... Rupert. Do you know what they want of us?"

"They want me to get you with child," Rupert's mind had been worrying at the conundrum. "I cannot puzzle out how that will be to their advantage."

He would have explored the topic some more, but Morris and Polly re-entered the room and began clearing the remnants of the meal.

"It is getting late, my lord," Morris said, "Soon be time for bed."

After helping him to strip and wash, Morris put a new shirt over Rupert's head and helped him into a banyan.

"You'll be wanting a shave, my lord," he said. A shave? Rupert had been shaved that morning before his wedding. But before he could open his mouth to contradict the servant, Morris went on, "You'll not want bristles when you kiss your lady, begging your pardon, my lord."

No. If Madeline's lips were as soft as her hands, bristles might scrape her skin. Whatever her role in the plot against him, and whatever that plot might be, Rupert did not want to hurt her. Rupert waved his permission, and spent the next few minutes, while Morris shaved him, considering what it might be like to kiss, to touch, the woman whose life was now joined to his. Since his mother died, he had only ever been touched by the impersonal hands of a servant.

What was about to happen would not be impersonal. He was going to… he thought of several vulgar words learnt from stable hands. The Old English Black horses bred at the Clearwater stud were the finest draught horses in the south of England, and Wyvern had insisted Rupert's infirmity did not prevent him from personally supervising the main activity of the enterprise.

Finished, Morris conducted him to the door between the dressing room and the bedchamber, where he could hear the maid bustling around. His wife must be here, too. Ah. Yes. He could smell her fragrance; hear her catch her breath at his entrance.

"Leave us," Rupert commanded, and waited, leaning against the doorframe, his head cocked to one side as he listened to the two servants retreating down the stairs. When he heard the heavy door between their prison and the rest of the castle shut and the external bolts being slid across, he broke the silence. "Are you nervous? I am nervous. I have never done this before."

"Nor have I," his wife ventured. She sounded uncertain.

"We do not have to, if you would rather not." It was the gentlemanly offer., however much he longed to explore the mysteries he had been denied by the strict care his guardian had seen fit to place around him.

She did not answer straight away, considering the suggestion. "We could pretend, I suppose. Do you think they will know if we do not…? Only Graviton said…" Her voice dropped so that even his keen ears strained to hear her. "Graviton said if you did not put a child in my belly, he would arrange for others to do so."

No one else would touch his countess. He would kill anyone who tried. Rupert made two attempts to speak before he could choke down his anger enough to speak calmly.

"We can wait, however, if you wish. Surely they will not know?"

"We cannot take that chance." Madeline was clearly more frightened of her brother than of their marriage night. In truth, whatever was good for the Ice Dragon and Graviton was probably very bad for the Earl and Countess of Penworth. But what choice did they have? His decision was plain sense, and nothing to do with the stirrings in his body.

He heard her cross to the bed and climb up into it, and after a moment, Rupert straightened and came too, shrugging off his banyan.

He slid under the covers and rolled to his side facing her, reaching out both hands. She met them with her own.

"Do you know what happens between a man and a woman, Madeline?" Rupert asked.

"Not exactly." Madeline sounded as if she were forcing herself to remain calm. "I breed dogs, but I do not suppose it is the same."

"No, not exactly the same." Rupert had been searching his memories of the pictures he'd found in the Clearwater library one long ago summer. He'd been thirteen at the time, and would have denied an interest, but studied them carefully and revisited them several times in the next weeks.

The man and woman faced one another in most of them, though other details of position changed. "Men and women mate with their fronts together," he told Madeline, doing his best to sound confident. "But I imagine much else is similar." He thought about the necessary steps when putting a stallion to a mare. "I should check first to see if you are receptive."

Her hands stiffened in his. Her voice shook slightly, and even in the silence of the room, he had to strain to hear it. "I … women don't come into heat. Do they?"

He was not certain, but listening to the banter of the grooms and footmen, he'd gained the impression some women were in heat all the time and others never. He hoped Madeline was not in the second category. Her tension was not a good sign. Perhaps he could soothe her, as he might a fractious mare.

"We don't have to do anything you don't like," he offered, and felt her hands ease slightly. "Madeline, may I 'see' you?"

"I do not understand."

"With my hands. May I touch you, so I can learn what you look like?"

Two

Madeline was not prepared for his gentleness.

Her new husband started with her hands, tracing each finger with one of his, skimming her palms, laying one of her hands atop his own and covering it with the other. Then he began to explore one arm; tentative trails with his fingertips become firmer sweeps, caresses, even. He circled her wrists with his hand. "How fine your bones are," he marvelled, his voice soft with awe. He brushed up the inner surface of her arm to her elbow. "Your skin; it is so soft."

His touch soothed and made her restless, both at the same time.

As he moved to hover over her, she rolled to her back, watching his face, intent and focused, turned slightly to one side, as if listening to the silent movement of his palms. He had beautiful eyes: dark brown with flecks of green and gold. The lamp she had left burning, reasoning that it made no difference to him, and would allow her to see, illuminated the side of his face and gilded his dark hair, leaving the other side in shadow.

The calluses on his violinist fingers set tingles running in her arm and in other, more private, places. How much of her did he plan to 'see'? She blushed at the thought, hoping the heat was not obvious to the man currently stroking high up her arms, his hands under the sleeves of her nightrail.

Perhaps he sensed her discomfort, because he slid the fabric down again, leaving her perversely wishing for the return of his touch. He moved to her face then, murmuring as he documented each of her features, and again, her skin tingled in the wake of his touch: her cheeks, her chin, her nose, one eye and then the other, the fingers gentle, barely touching the lids, her lips, once, twice, three times, and back again, until her lips twitched with the effort of not kissing the sweet tormentors.

He traced her ears, stroking up to push away the mob cap she wore over her neatly plaited hair. "One day, I wish to run my hands through this silky fineness," he said, and she shivered at the thought.

Rupert hesitated, his fingers stopping their gentle massage of her scalp. "You don't like the idea?"

Her own voice was unfamiliar, breathless and thready. "I do not mind. If you wish." She could imagine it, and her whole scalp longed for it. But how could she tell him that?

"Help me, Madeline," Rupert pleaded. "Tell me what you like and what you do not like. I cannot see your face. I guess at what you are thinking and feeling, but I cannot know, unless you tell me."

"I…" She swallowed and tried again. "I cannot speak when you are touching me so, Rupert. I can barely think. I—I like it. I like it very much." Surely, he could feel the heat of her blush, hovering over her face as he was, those magical fingers moving again down the sides of her cheeks.

Greatly daring, she put her own hand up to cup one side of his face, and he turned into it, kissing her palm and sending a bolt of sensation down her arm and into her core.

"Too much?" Rupert asked, anxiously.

"I like it," Madeline repeated. She wasn't sure it was true. Her skin, wherever his hands had roamed, felt thinner than it had ever been, as if his touch had stripped off several layers and left her near-raw, sensitive to slight shifts in the bedchamber's air.

He smiled in answer and caught her hand in his, kissing the palm again, then her wrist and up her forearm to her elbow.

Abruptly, he sat back, letting one hand trail down her side, over her hip, and down her leg to her foot. Then he began as he had with her hands, exploring each foot in turn, following up past the ankle to the knee until her legs, too, were yearning. And all the time, he described how she felt to his touch, exclaiming with wonder at her softness, her curves, the chilliness of her toes, which he amended by putting them, one by one, into his mouth.

"I like it," she managed again, when he stopped to make the query, and he continued, scraping his teeth experimentally, but gently, against the ball of her big toe. How peculiar. She felt the scrape all the way down her torso, deep inside, like an itch, but sweeter. How would it feel if he touched her there, in that private place where the sweetness centred?

Rupert was reaching further up under her nightrail now, and she shifted restlessly, embarrassed, but also hoping he would continue all the way up. But the nightrail's billowing fullness was in his way.

"What do you call this thing?" he asked, as he tried to roll the hem. "Can we take it off? It is a nuisance."

If she took off her nightrail, she would be naked. But her reasoning when she decided to leave the lamp lit still applied. There was no one here to see. Not even her husband, who surely had the right to remove her garments if he chose?

No. She could not do it. Not while he wore a nightshirt.

The answer was obvious.

"I will if you will," she told him, and without a word, he sat back on his heels, pulled his shirt over his head, and tossed it behind him on the floor.

In moments, they were both naked. Madeline hardly noticed the chill of the night air bringing goosebumps to her arms as she gaped at her new husband. She had known, of course, that men were different than women. He was angular where she was curved, his shoulders broad and muscular, his chest tightly defined planes. Where her skin was smooth and bare, his bore dark hair in the shape of a rough cross, the horizontal reaching from side to side, the vertical arrowing down to...

Her mouth dried as her eyes followed to where the line pointed. More dark curls, and among them, thicker and longer than she expected, his... Her kennel master called it a pizzle, but no dog had one that size! Of course, dogs were smaller altogether, and puppies, too, much smaller than a human child, and some people clearly enjoyed what was about to occur if the scandalous behaviour at harvest time could be taken in evidence.

Lady Wyvern, too, undoubtedly allowed Graviton… So it wasn't just the lower orders, and why would it be? A pedigree showed no more discretion than a mongrel when in heat, and the kennel hands needed to be alert to keep a determined bitch confined so she didn't…

He was reaching for her again, and all the words chattering on in her head tumbled to silence when she dragged her fascinated gaze upward to his intent face.

"May I?" He was asking for permission to touch her, and his courtesy was reassuring. Suddenly bold, she moved forward so his hands encountered her left arm and her right breast, and she put her own hands deliberately on his chest. Husbands could touch wives, of course. But surely wives could also touch husbands?

Rupert froze. She had her hands on him, resting softly on his body, just above his nipples. Would she move them? Would she explore him as he did her? Oh, he hoped so! He set the example, stroking his hand down her arm to the elbow and then inward, to curve around her waist and draw her nearer, at the same time cupping whatever his other hand had fallen upon. Her breast, it must be. It filled his hand beautifully, and the skin was soft, like warm satin, like the nose of a new-born foal.

The scent of citrus teased his nostrils again, and he bent closer to inhale. Yes. It was her hair. "You smell of lemons and violets," he murmured, hardly aware he was speaking, with so much of his mind absorbed in documenting the feel of her skin, of her curves, and revelling in the slow, halting movements of her hands as she shaped the muscles of his chest, his shoulders, his upper arms, then back to his chest.

Where would she touch next? His own hand traced the flare of her hips, then reached further to curve his long fingers around one buttock, as his other hand continued to stroke the breast, brushing over the… did they call it a teat in a woman? No. Nipple. It was a nipple. He took it between two fingers and rubbed gently, and Madeline squirmed, rubbing up against him.

She spoke, her voice sounding as distracted as he felt. "My hair."

"Mmmm?" What about her hair? He reluctantly let go of her breast and felt his way up the side of her face to run his fingers into her hair. It was silky and fine, and stray tendrils clung to his skin, escaped from the tight plait.

"I perfume the soap with oil of violets and use lemon verbena in the rinse water," Madeline explained. His question. She was answering the question he had forgotten asking.

He let his hand drift down to her breast again, and she shivered as it ran over her naked skin. He should tell her what he wanted, but if he asked her to take his shaft in her hands, she might be offended. He should be more subtle, perhaps. "Do you like that? I like the way you are touching me."

"I like it," she repeated.

Coaxing her to describe what she liked, asking her specific questions, telling her how her hands felt on his chest, his flanks, his arms—it excited him further but, paradoxically, helped him to keep from flinging himself on top of her. Mating had its own rhythm, just as music did, and his wife was not a mare to correct him with her teeth and hooves if he rushed her. He would need to repeat the same *motifs* in all their variant forms until the symphony reached its exposition, the fulfilment of the primary melody.

At his gentle urging, she became bolder, and firmer in her strokes, her hands tending closer to what he hoped would be their goal.

As he caressed her, he formed an image in his mind. She was small, much smaller than he, and curved in interesting ways, from her soft arms to the globes of her breasts, bigger than he expected, but still small enough for him to cup with one hand. Below the breasts, her body narrowed to a tiny waist he could span with his long fingers, and then flared out again. He brushed his hand across the soft curls he found in the spot he yearned for. He had curls in the same place, but otherwise, she was completely different.

Kissing her behind the ear, which made her squirm with what he hoped was pleasure, he dipped a finger down from the curls into the one part of her body he had not explored. She was warm and wet, and he was fascinated by the folds of skin he found. Completely different.

She pushed herself against him when he found the place he would soon be filling. The part he would use was throbbing and twitching with eagerness. He would spend if he did not soon enter her, and his tutor had always assured him that spending, except as God commanded—in marriage and in one's wife—was a wicked sin that would send him to hell. Well, now he had a wife, and she was ready, surely?

"Are you ready?" he asked, just to be certain.

"Rupert," she answered, pushing herself still harder, and he took that as a yes, lifting himself over her. He guided his tip to her entrance and then could wait no longer. With a surge, he was fully seated, and it felt wonderful. Better than he had imagined.

He had plunged several times before he realised she was not moving. With a mighty effort, he froze in place. "Madeline? Are you all right?" She was rigid below him, and though the tightness felt wonderful, he did not think she was enjoying it.

"It hurts," she said, voice trembling with tears.

"I'm sorry." He made to pull out, cursing the ignorance that had caused him to hurt this little wife he had somehow acquired. But she held onto him, both hands gripping his hips.

"No. It is feeling better now. I am not... Stay. Please."

And because he wanted to, he let himself be persuaded, but held as still as he could while he kissed her, horrified to find her cheeks wet under his searching lips.

"I hurt you," he grieved, and again tried to pull away. Again, she held him in place. "I am better, Rupert. It feels good. Please stay."

He rested his weight on his elbows, caged her face with his hands, and covered her with kisses, trying to focus on the meeting of their lips while his hips trembled with the need to surge and pump.

She met him with her own lips, pressing little kisses all over his face, and after a long moment, he could feel the tension in her ease. Slowly, cautiously, ready to clamp the iron control back over the animal within, he eased slightly away and then back. Again. And again.

When she began tentatively lifting her hips to meet his thrusts, he could hold himself in check no longer. His body took over as his mind, his sensations, his whole universe narrowed to the heaven of the elusive, approaching, present, completed release.

Madeline could feel when Rupert finished. He took much longer than a dog, but stiffened in the same way, staying rigid for half a minute before rolling to his side, holding her, so she came with him. "Are you... I did not mean to hurt you, Madeline. Are you well?"

"I am well," she assured him. "It only hurt for a moment. It was nothing, truly."

"But was it pleasant for you?" he asked. This concern surprised and pleased her. He was not at all the top-lofty aristocrat she had been expecting. She responded to the anxiety in his tone and thought about his question.

It had been something of an anti-climax. The size of him had made her wary. Then the wonderful sensations he had evoked while caressing her had led her to expect pleasure, so the first sharp pain had come as a shock. But once she relaxed, it had not been as uncomfortable as she had feared. On the whole, it had been rather pleasant. Strange, but pleasant.

"Yes, it was," she assured him. "And for you?"

His voice was awed, as if he had participated in a miracle. "It was wonderful. I had no idea. Can we do it again later?"

They slept, and then coupled, then slept again. The third time, the sense of something more seemed almost within reach—but then he finished and, once again, rolled to his side, holding her against him. It was pleasant lying in his arms. She had not been held with affection since her mother had died when she was ten. The candle had long since guttered, but the dawn light showed his face relaxed in sleep. His face was all she could see, since he had pulled the blanket up to cover them. She lay studying him, as if she had to commit him to memory and would be examined on the subject after she broke her fast.

She was considering the stubble now darkening his cheeks when he spoke. "Good morning, madam wife."

"Good morning, my lord," she answered, a smile bubbling in her voice. He was awake and surely would not mind if she did as she wished. She brushed the beginnings of his beard. "It prickles," she discovered.

"I will have Morris shave me again this morning," Rupert promised.

"No need. I like the way it looks."

"I do not wish to scrape your skin, Madeline, when I kiss you. You are so soft and tender." He rolled again, caging her with his arms and body. "And I do wish to kiss you. Very soon and very often." Carefully, he lowered his head and brushed her face lightly with his lips, then rubbed his rough skin gently against her cheek.

"Are you well? Are you recovered from the hurt?" He had asked her that twice in the night, each time before he took her again. She spread her legs obligingly, but he said, "No. I must clean myself and shave. And let you recover, for though you say you are not in pain, I fear you say so just to please me. Tell me the truth, Madeline. Are you well? Do you still hurt?"

She thought about it. She ached a little, the ache of exerting little-used muscles. And she was sticky. She, too, would welcome a wash. But she could tell him honestly, "I do not hurt, Rupert. I would like a bath, though."

"It is a messy business, is it not?" he said, cheerfully, shifting to lie beside her, her head cradled on his arm.

"What do you wish to do today? I shall practise a little, of course, but we could... I do not know your interests or how you normally spend the day."

"At home, I manage the household, see to my dogs, read, sew or knit or practice my music."

His face sharpened with interest. "You sing? Or you play an instrument?"

"The spinet. I play the spinet and sing a little."

"Then we shall ask for a spinet, so you can practise. I will ask, but I think they will not let us have your dogs, Madeline. I am sorry. Are there books here in the tower for you to read?"

She had seen none. "I do not think so, Rupert."

"Then we shall ask for books, too, or permission for you to go to Lord Wyvern's library and choose your own."

"Surely now you are wed... Rupert, you are the Earl of Penworth. You do not need permission, do you? And now that you are wed, you are considered of age." Or so the author had claimed in the horrid novel she had read just a few weeks ago. "How old are you, Rupert?"

"Twenty. I shall be twenty-one in a few months. But it makes no difference, Madeline. Lady Wyvern and Lord Graviton rule here, and we are their prisoners."

"She is your sister. Surely she does not mean you harm?"

Rupert's response was bitter. "Half-sister, and she has hated me all my life. She would harm me if it were to her advantage, but while I live—and with Lord Wyvern absent—she has the whole earldom at her command."

The thought that flashed into Madeline's mind was so Gothic she hesitated to give voice to it, but Rupert's mind had clearly gone in the same direction. "While I live…" he repeated.

"If we have a child…"

"If he is a son…"

Madeline turned into him, stretching her arm across his chest, as if she could shield him from the malice. "Then we must avoid making a child."

He returned the hug, kissing her hair. "It will not answer, Madeline. Perhaps Graviton might hesitate to carry out his threat—his own sister, after all. But the Ice Dragon will not care who fathers my heir, as long as someone does. We cannot trust your brother to protect you."

She shivered. "Half-brother. And he has hated me all his life."

"Well, then." He gave her a squeeze and another kiss. "We have time. They will keep me for my stud services until they have a boy child. Two, if they are wise."

She scooted up, so her return kiss could reach his lips. "We will find a way to escape, and we will go to the king!" They would have a year. Or perhaps two or three years. Surely, in that time, they could foil their captors?

"Or Lord Wyvern might return," Rupert said, hopefully, but Madeline did not intend to count on that chance.

Three

When they went downstairs to break their fast, Rupert proclaimed himself keen to show Madeline the smoothness of his freshly shaven cheeks, and she found herself sitting on his knee, popping pieces of fruit, bread roll, and bacon into his mouth, or her own, in between kisses.

How strange at this time yesterday, she and Graviton were on the mainland, in a carriage to the wharf, where a boat waited to bring them to Wyvern Island. She had not even met Rupert! She could scarcely believe they were so comfortable with one another in such a short time.

She spoke her thoughts out loud, and he agreed. "I only thought of keeping my lady safe," he confessed. "I never thought of what marriage would mean."

Madeline blushed, thinking he meant their intimacies. She could not have imagined how peculiar and awkward the activity would be—nice though it was.

Rupert, though, had another pleasure in mind. "I have not had a companion of my own age since the accident when I lost my sight," he confided. "I think we shall be friends, Madeline. I would like that."

She blushed still more, and hid her hot face against his neck. "I would like that, too. I have never had a friend. Except for my dogs."

They were interrupted by the sound of bolts being drawn back on the door below them. Madeline wriggled, and Rupert let her out of his arms to take her own seat, next to him, around the corner of the table.

Lady Wyvern swept into the room, Graviton sauntering behind her. "Well, Penworth? Did you do your duty?" she demanded.

Under the table top, Madeline slipped her hand into Rupert's, and he pressed it reassuringly.

"You are early, sister," he said, his chin lifted and jaw rigid.

"No need for concern, Louisa," Graviton soothed. He smirked at Madeline and Robert. "Our newly-weds are holding hands under the table. It is rather sweet."

Lady Wyvern was not amused. "But did he bed her, James? Holding hands won't fill her belly."

"He did, my lady." It was the maid, Polly, shrinking a little as she drew the attention of everyone in the room.

"Explain," Lady Wyvern demanded, and Polly shrank still further, looking around as if for support. Her uncle spoke for her. "Blood on the sheets, my lady. He popped her cherry, right enough."

Lady Wyvern glared, and her voice was cold, "You will speak to and of the earl and countess with all due respect, Morris, or I will replace you and your niece."

"Beg pardon, my lady." Morris said something else, but Madeline was not listening. Turning to Rupert as the grip on her hand tightened, she found his face white. "I made you bleed?" he asked, in a low voice meant for her ears only.

But Graviton heard. "No need to fuss, Penworth. She'll be fine next time." Madeline blushed and instinctively turned to Rupert, searching his still-anxious face. Graviton began to snigger. "Ah. Next time has been. From the looks of my dear little sister, Louisa, he bedded her several times."

"Curse you, Graviton." The earl's voice was harsh and imperious, making him sound much older. "Hold your tongue. You are being offensive."

Madeline flinched. Graviton's temper was uncertain, and though Rupert was tall, Graviton had a man's full growth. But Graviton only laughed. "The puppy thinks he is a man, now," he observed.

"Do not tease them, James," Lady Wyvern commanded. "We are pleased, are we not? You shall have a reward, Penworth, you and your countess. I shall instruct the servants to make your stay here comfortable. You may ask for anything, within reason."

"Our freedom," Rupert said, but that made Lord Graviton chortle still harder and Lady Wyvern frown.

"Within reason, Penworth. Music, perhaps, so you don't have to pick out your own on your infernal violin? The countess has been trained to read music, James, I take it?"

"Mad has been trained as a lady, Louisa; of course she reads music. She plays tolerably well, too." Madeline had had the best of teachers while Papa was alive, though nothing these last five years. Graviton had fired them all, saying he had no intention of parading her on the marriage market, but would place her where suited him best.

"There, Penworth. You shall have some sheet music, and your little wife shall play for you. Come, James. We do not wish to miss the boat."

As the couple started to leave, Rupert stopped them with a word: "Wait."

Lady Wyvern turned back, slapping the gloves she held in one hand impatiently against the other. "Well? Be quick, Penworth."

"Lady Penworth's spinet, access to Lord Wyvern's library, Lady Penworth's favourite dog, a walk outside in clement weather. And the music."

Lady Wyvern exchanged looks with Graviton. "The countess may have her spinet. You and she shall not leave the tower. A servant shall fetch whatever books she desires. I have already agreed to the music."

"And the dog?" Rupert insisted.

"James? What think you?"

Graviton was shaking his head. "No, Louisa. A dog in this tower? With those stairs? We would not wish any harm to come to the earl."

"Maera would never trip my husband," Madeline protested. "Never."

"No dog," Lady Wyvern decreed. "Morris, we will send the other things. See to it the earl and countess are treated as befits their station."

She left as abruptly as she had arrived, and Graviton followed her, turning in the doorway to grin at Madeline. "You were worth keeping after all, Mad," he said. "I did think about selling you when Father died, but this is much better."

Second movement: Adagio

Four

The tower was a comfortable cage. Sometimes it seemed to Madeline she had lived here forever, talking with Rupert for hours on end, reading to him from the books Polly collected in bundles from the library—or at least from those books that were suitable, since Polly was just as likely to bring an account book or something in a language Madeline did not know—making music and making love. Rupert was nearly as startled as Madeline when she reached her first climax, but he quickly learnt how to play her body with the dedicated attention to detail, and the flair, that he applied to his violin.

Her world, always limited to the estate of Graviton Manor and the nearby village, had shrunk to the three upper floors of this tower.

At Graviton, she been surrounded by people: servants, villagers, neighbours. Here, had it not been for the occasional voices of guards when the doors were opening for Morris or Polly to come or go, or the sight of people crossing the courtyard in view of the tower windows, she might have thought she and Rupert and the two servants were the only people in the world. And the tower ghost, of course, the White Lady of Wyvern.

The White Lady was something of a joke between them, since they had seen no hint of the lost and bewildered lady who had purportedly died here, bricked up by her jealous husband who had, a few months later, tripped down the stairs into a dungeon cell and broken his neck. He was there yet, the servants whispered, trapped forever in the dungeons, and never able to reach and make amends to his wronged lady in the upper reaches of the castle they had shared.

At Graviton, Madeline had often been lonely. Here, she never was. She and Rupert were rarely apart, even by the length of a flight of stairs. They loved the same music. They largely agreed on the types of books they liked, and had fun arguing when they disagreed. They shared stories of their childhoods, which were remarkably similar.

Both were only children of second marriages, with mothers resented by the adult children of the first marriage. Both had been raised in the country, separated by their noble status from neighbours of the same age, surrounded by adult servants. Both had lost their mothers when they were ten.

Rupert's father had died in the same epidemic of ague that killed his mother. At least Madeline had kept her father until her eighteenth year. He had indulged his daughter with tutors and books, but kept her largely isolated until he died, at which point, she became a dependent of the new baronet, her half-brother, Sir James Graviton, who spent most of his time in London and largely ignored her.

Rupert, on the death of his parents, had become the ward of his half-brother, the new earl, who had also lived in London—with occasional visits to Clearwater for the hunting. Rupert had been most often confined to the nursery wing, while the earl filled his house with friends and hangers-on, ignoring the unwanted younger brother.

And then the 6th Earl of Penworth had died. Rupert could not tell Madeline the details. He had been injured in the same accident, suffering such a blow to the back of his head that he was also expected to die. "Nobody knows why I was with my brother in the phaeton. He had never before invited me to drive with him. And I cannot remember." Rupert was found, unconscious, thrown clear of the crushed remains of the carriage that had failed to take the turn at the gate. The earl was dead in the wreckage.

After days hovering between life and death, and months of headaches, Rupert recovered his senses, but not his sight. This did not deter his new guardian, his father's best friend and his sister's husband. Lord Wyvern set about training the young earl in the duties of his new position.

Rupert spoke of his guardian with respect and affection, but Madeline thought his life sounded very regimented and constrained.

He was educated according to his station, memorising his lessons, since he could not write them. When not in the schoolroom, he was expected to attend to the business of the earldom, at first listening as Lord Wyvern explored the options and made decisions, and slowly taking over one small part of the work of one estate, then more and more.

Lady Wyvern seldom accompanied her lord to Clearwater, where Rupert had grown up, and paid her sole remaining brother little attention when she did.

"These last few years, she usually had your brother with her when she came," Rupert said. "Why did Lord Wyvern allow it?"

"Were they lovers even then?" Madeline asked.

"The servants thought so."

They were in the upper part of the tower. Since the day Rupert imperiously banned Morris and Polly from setting foot inside the topmost room, it had become their favourite place. Madeline kept the place tidy and dusted, much to Polly's veiled amusement. Rupert overheard her calling Madeline 'the countess of cleaning,' but she showed no open disrespect, and was endlessly willing to fetch books, wool, or most other things Madeline requested, so Madeline ignored the remark.

Polly became her devoted handmaid the day Madeline realised the eclectic array of books were a symptom of Polly's inability to read, and offered to teach the maid her letters.

So, Polly willingly obeyed the ban on entering the music room, and Morris did so with a smirk, whispering to Polly that the couple wanted privacy for 'making them babies her ladyship wants.' "And none of her ladyship's business what the poor lambs do," Polly retorted. "I'll not spy on them, and you shouldn't neither."

The servants were not entirely wrong about why Rupert and Madeline wanted privacy. They were currently reclining on the large, comfortable sofa, resting after making love, which, in turn, followed a particularly vigorous practice session on a new concerto that had been in this month's sheet music bundle from London.

Soon, Rupert would dress and fetch the tray of food that was, undoubtedly, by now out on the landing, on a table set there for the purpose. Then Rupert would practice again, and Madeline would knit.

The knitting was the primary reason for the ban. From time to time, Madeline would bring down a completed pair of gloves or stockings for her wardrobe or Rupert's, or a baby's singlet or shawl or mittens, to be carefully wrapped in paper and set into a slowly filling chest.

She had no idea who received her written requests for different colours, types, and quantities of yarn, but—so far, at least— whoever it was had not thought to question Polly about the garments that appeared downstairs, or to calculate the difference between the quantity of wool that went into the upper room, and the quantity she used.

That difference was a multi-coloured, multi-textured ladder, slowly growing from between her needles.

She and Rupert had trialled it, tossing it over the rafters that supported the tower roof, and hanging on it to see how far it stretched, so they could measure the length needed. In four months, the ladder had grown nearly long enough to reach the ground in the courtyard.

Perhaps, in another week, it would do? And, of course, they would need the right weather and tides to steal a boat and safely cross to the mainland. The island had once been accessible at low tide, Rupert told her, but the half-mile causeway had washed away centuries ago, and storms could close the channel for days at a time.

They would also need to wait until the courtyard was empty. The seaward side of the tower was too dangerous, they had decided, with a sheer cliff to breakers below.

Rupert dropped a kiss on the top of her head. "Are you hungry, madam wife?"

She nodded. She was always hungry now, making up for the few weeks when food would not stay down.

"Sit up, then," her husband said, "and I will fetch the tray."

She watched him cross the room and go out the door. No onlooker would have believed him blind. He walked with confident ease in this space he knew so well. As long as she made sure everything remained in its place, he had a mental map of their entire three-floor domain, and he needed no help to move freely around it.

Once they were free, she would train a dog to go everywhere with him, like the dog she had seen leading a blind gypsy at a fair. He would be able to go anywhere, then.

He was back quickly, placing the heavy tray on the table where they ate their meals.

"Come here, Madeline," he said, "and feed my son."

"Or your daughter," she reminded him. She hoped the baby was a girl. A girl would win her husband a reprieve. But it would not come to that. It could not be allowed to come to that. She would keep knitting until the ladder was long enough, and they would escape.

Soon. Soon they would make their bid for freedom. Before the storms of winter. Before she was too bulky to climb down the twisting, turning concoction of threads on which they had hung their hopes.

Soon.

Third movement: Allegro

Five

Before they could put their plan into action, Lady Wyvern and Lord Graviton returned. The castle had been unsettled for several days, with more boats than usual crossing to and from the mainland, and a veritable army of maids coming and going from the tower on the other side of the courtyard. They were cleaning, Madeline concluded, watching one staggering in through the door under a yoke of buckets.

Morris, when asked, denied anything was different, and Polly giggled, her usual response to a question she was forbidden to answer.

When their captors arrived, Madeline and Rupert were in their sanctuary, Madeline knitting while he played his violin. The sound of more than two pairs of feet on the stairs alerted Rupert to the danger.

"Madeline, hide the ladder," he hissed, an urgent whisper, not ceasing his playing, and she scrambled to thrust it into the chest beside her, regaining her seat with another set of needles and a half-finished baby bonnet just as Lady Wyvern and Lord Graviton entered—without first knocking.

Rupert glowered as he kept playing. Madeline's first reaction was to stand, but she reminded herself she outranked them both, and remained seated. The knitting helped keep her hands steady, and her voice was deceptively calm as she said, "Lady Wyvern, Graviton." She inclined her head graciously, as she imagined a countess ought to do.

Lady Wyvern's nostrils flared, but she returned the greeting: "Lady Penworth."

"Please be seated," Madeline managed, moments before Lady Wyvern sat without invitation. Graviton, though, prowled the room, picking things up and putting them down. How dare he invade their space and handle their things? Madeline commanded her body not to shake, her trembling now as much anger as fear.

Rupert was on the second and final movement of the piece he had been playing. Lady Wyvern regarded him with open dislike, then turned her frown on Madeline, talking loudly to be heard over the music. "Morris informs me the two of you spend most of your time up here. How can you stand the racket Penworth makes?"

"His Lordship is very talented," Madeline replied. "I am privileged to hear him."

"Hmm." Lady Wyvern did not sound convinced. The smile she plastered on did not reach her eyes. "You are fortunate to find it so. What is that you are knitting, countess? Something for the baby?"

Madeline did not believe the pleasantries for a moment, but she responded in kind, holding out the half-finished cap, knitting needles and all. "A cap, Lady Wyvern."

Lady Wyvern gave it a cursory glance. "Yes. Very nice. Very suitable."

Graviton leaned against the back of Lady Wyvern's chair, brushing her neck with his fingers. "Yes, yes. I am sure we all want to sit around all afternoon being entertained by your brother and admiring my sister's industry, while the King's man snoops to his heart's delight."

Rupert kept playing, but Madeline, who had heard this particular sonata many times, caught the slight misstep that indicated he had heard.

"The King's man is thinking of nothing but his bath and a rest before dinner, my dear James," Lady Wyvern scolded. "We have time to coach Lord and Lady Penworth in their part. And Penworth will not give us his full attention if he is not allowed to finish."

Graviton pushed away and circled the room again, pacing with short, jerky steps, as if he could not contain his energy.

"How long?" he barked at Madeline. A matter of seconds, as it happened. Rupert was on the final bars, as anyone whose ears were not made of cloth could have heard. Not that she would say that. In their few encounters since her father had died, most of them on the journey here to Wyvern Castle, Madeline had learned to be wary of her brother's reaction when anything touched his pride.

Rupert drew the bow to a lingering halt and stood, letting the vibrating strings fill the room with the last, sweet notes of the *motif*. Then, still seemingly ignoring their visitors, he crossed to the table where the violin case lay.

"Sir James shifted the case several inches to the right and rear, my lord." Madeline would not call her husband by his personal name in front of these invaders. Rupert, who was lowering the violin over the table, changed his stance and swung it to the new position, fumbling very little as he fitted it into the shaped lining.

"Thank you, my lady." Rupert crossed to sit on the chest beside Madeline, where he could hold the hand she slipped into his, and also prevent Graviton's restless explorations from disclosing Madeline's knitting.

"Very well, Lady Wyvern. What do you want of us?" Rupert's voice was calm. Only the stickiness of his palm betrayed his emotions.

"Straight to the point, Penworth? No greetings for your sister?"

Rupert raised his eyebrows, his head turned in the direction of Lady Wyvern's voice, for all the world as if he could see her.

"You like me as little as I like you, Sister." He almost spat the last word, lip curling with disdain. "So let us not waste time on meaningless social niceties."

Graviton returned to his post at Lady Wyvern's shoulder, chuckling. "He has you there, Louisa. Damned if I don't almost like the boy!"

Lady Wyvern scowled, though Graviton gave no sign of noticing. Madeline gripped Rupert's hand a little tighter. His blindness gave him some advantages.

"Very well. If you will insist on being barbarians. We have a visitor. Lord Morpeth. We need the two of you to attend dinner with him this evening and meet with him tomorrow. Perhaps more than once. Graviton or I will always be present during such meetings, and we will instruct you on what you are to say."

"And what you are not to say," Graviton added.

Rupert remained silent, leaving Madeline to ask, "What is the purpose of Lord Morpeth's visit?"

For a moment, she thought Lady Wyvern would not answer, but after exchanging glances with Graviton, the older woman condescended to explain, "I imagine you will hear it from Morpeth. Very well. Now that Lord Penworth is twenty-one, the king has decided to find out whether he is fit for his duties to the earldom, given his blindness. Your condition will help us, countess, though I could wish the babe born and a son." She shrugged. "Still, what we have in mind should suffice."

"And if I am unfit?" Rupert asked.

"Then you are of no more use to us," Graviton hissed, low and vicious. "If you are unfit, we have no more need of you. And accidents can happen very easily to a man without sight."

Madeline clutched convulsively at Rupert's hand, though she tried to show no other sign of her alarm. He was lying, of course. They did not need Rupert to run the earldom they had already taken from him. Rather, they needed him, and Madeline, to provide heirs to legitimise their trusteeship of the estates.

"Accidents can happen even more easily to a violin," Lady Wyvern purred. "You are fit to be earl, Penworth, or so my husband assured me. You will parade your knowledge of estate management, the interconnections between noble families, and the wellbeing of the kingdom, and you will not, by any word or action, alert Lord Morpeth to any irregularities in your situation. Your current accommodations are comfortable, but they could easily become less so. You have your violin and the company of your wife. That will change, I assure you, if you do not cooperate."

Rupert made a derisory noise. "By 'irregularities,' you refer to the fact you are keeping me and my wife prisoner, and have—in effect—stolen my estates? That you intend to keep me at stud until you have a child to make earl in my place?"

Graviton laughed again. "You said he was smart, Louisa. Yes, *my lord*," he gave the title a sarcastic twist. "That is precisely what we mean by irregularities." His smile gone, as if it had never been, he leaned forward, enunciating each word precisely. "Make no mistake, Penworth. Appealing to Morpeth will do you only harm. He would be easy to convince that your accident left you mad. Wyvern's protectiveness has done you no favours there. No one knows you. No one can speak for you. And if your grieving sister reluctantly concedes that you must be locked up for your own good and the estates held in trust for your heir, well, who is to know or care, after Morpeth leaves, whether your prison is this tower or Wyvern's dungeons? Or worse?"

The servants, Madeline thought. But they are Lady Wyvern's creatures.

Lady Wyvern stood. "You will be escorted to dinner when it is time, Penworth, countess. Come, James. We should bathe and change for dinner." She stopped on her way to the door. "Lord Wyvern will not be joining us this evening, but you may prepare yourself to see him in the next few days, once he is able to entertain visitors."

"He lives?" Rupert dropped Madeline's hand to start after his sister, who curved her lips though her eyes remained cold.

"Oh, yes. He lives. He has been ill, Penworth, but he lives."

"He is more useful that way," Graviton observed, "for the present."

Rupert had time for a hurried consultation with his wife before they separated to place themselves in the hands of the servants to be, as Madeline put it, transformed into an earl and countess to impress the King's man. They would need to comply with their jailers' commands, at least until they saw a chance to convince Morpeth of their plight. If they could. Lord Wyvern had not taken Rupert to meet his peers, but Rupert had been expected to learn all about them. Lord Wyvern had described the Earl of Morpeth as both conservative and stupid.

Escorted to the parlour by Morris and a phalanx of strapping footmen, Rupert was able to form his own judgement. Morpeth, on being presented to Rupert and Madeline, immediately turned to Graviton to gush, "But she is charming, my dear baron. Charming."

And then, to Rupert, "I must congratulate you, Lord Penworth. I imagine you do not know how fortunate you are. Young men so often do not appreciate their wives as they should, I find. Now, let me help you be seated, Penworth." He insisted on taking Rupert by the arm to lead him to a chair, turning him and pushing at his hips. "Sit, Penworth. Sit. I have you safe."

"Once the ladies are seated, my lord," Rupert insisted. "Lady Penworth?"

In the past four months, her lack of training for this role had not mattered, but unexpectedly, they were in company, and she was the highest-ranked lady in the room, Rupert's title being older than Wyvern's. He smiled in the direction he had last heard her, trying to project his confidence in her.

"Please be seated, Lady Wyvern, gentlemen." Her voice sounded calm and assured. Rupert's smile broadened. She would manage.

Morpeth demanded his attention again. "Charming," he repeated. "Such a lovely young woman. And Lady Wyvern tells me she is already doing her duty to the title and to you, Penworth. You must be very pleased."

Rupert was tempted to tell the fussy, old bore to mind his own business, but he murmured something bland, and soon, Morpeth was chattering about happenings in London and abroad, managing the conversation so well by himself that Rupert could pay only half attention, listening all the time to hear what the Ice Dragon and her lover were saying to Madeline.

Commonplaces about the weather, it seemed, and not for long, as the butler appeared at the door, making only the faintest of sounds to alert Rupert before Madeline said, "Dinner is served my lady, gentlemen. Shall we go through?"

"A nice problem," Morpeth commented. "Four gentlemen and only two ladies. Do two men each escort one lady, Penworth? Hey?"

"I will exercise the privilege of a man yet on his bridal tour, and take in my own wife," Rupert said firmly. "See that we are seated together, please."

"Penworth, you will disrupt my table," Lady Wyvern complained.

"Indulge me in this, Sister?" Madeline asked, sweetly. "My lord and I have not been parted by as much as a table length these four months." She crossed the room and placed her hand in the one Rupert held up to receive it.

"How delightful." From the sound of his voice, Morpeth was beaming. He was, as Lord Wyvern had described, a sentimentalist, as well as a bombastic fool.

"Yes. Very sweet." Lady Wyvern was anything but pleased, but the orders she gave to the butler were in her best interests, too. With Madeline at his side to direct him, he could creditably manage a meal he could not see, and with him to advise her, she would conduct herself as a countess should.

"You said four gentlemen, Lord Morpeth," Rupert said, once they were seated. "A fourth gentleman has not been presented to me?" He made the last sentence into a question, and Morpeth stumbled over an apology.

"An oversight, I assure you. Only my secretary, Penworth. May I present Mr Davin Umbra."

"My lord." The secretary's voice came from beyond Madeline, who sat to Rupert's left. It was low, slightly husky, and definitely amused. At Rupert? At the man's master?

"Mr Umbra, my dear," Rupert said to Madeline, taking some pleasure in discomfiting Morpeth for neglecting to present the man to them both.

"An unusual name, Mr Umbra. It is Latin for 'shadow,' is it not? Yet, you sound English?" Madeline said.

"I am indeed, my lady, although I have some Italian blood on my father's side."

"You understand a little Latin, countess?" Morpeth asked, both incredulous and condescending.

"Lady Penworth has a superior understanding," Rupert told him, which made Morpeth chuckle.

"It does my heart good to hear you say so, Penworth. It does, indeed. When the King told me you were wed, and asked me to come see if there were anything suspicious about it, well, I do not mind telling you I wondered what I would find. But it is easy to see she dotes on you, and you on her."

This was true, Rupert thought, but hardly to the point. Obedient to his sister's command, though, he did not comment.

"No, Lord Morpeth," Madeline said firmly, interrupting whatever Morpeth was about to say next. "You will allow me to serve my husband, although you may hold the dishes, if you will. Lord Penworth, let me explain what is on offer."

She proceeded to describe each dish and serve a portion of those Rupert selected. Each time, she told him where he would find it on his plate, using the clock-face analogy they had developed together over many meals. "Your large spoonful of ragout is at three of the clock, next to the mashed parsnip and carrot at five of the clock."

With the mental picture she helped him form, he had no need to run his hand over the plate, but could confidently use his cutlery to eat like a gentleman.

Morpeth was very impressed and exclaimed over their system, but was soon diverted into speaking of London gossip with Graviton and Lady Wyvern. When he applied to Rupert for an opinion, Rupert told him, "My wife and I have not seen a newspaper these four months, Lord Morpeth."

Morpeth chuckled. "More important business, hey? More important business. Never you mind, boy… I mean, Penworth. You have been applying yourself with some effect!"

Madeline's hand crept onto Rupert's knee under the table, and he put his own hand down to give hers a squeeze. What a rude old man.

"Wyvern Castle is an unusual place," said Umbra, breaking the subsequent tense silence. "It must have been easy to defend in the old days."

Rupert seized the change of topic. "There was a causeway until the sixteenth century. You can still see some remnants at spring tide."

"Now, the only access is by boat," Lady Wyvern complained. "And not at all in a storm."

"The causeway was only accessible at low tide," Rupert told her. Lord Wyvern had told him the history of the castle many times.

"It was never taken by an enemy force from without, though it has twice been lost by betrayal from within," he went on. Once in the Civil War, and once—if he was not mistaken—this last year, when Lady Wyvern took it from its rightful lord to bestow on the man cuckolding him.

Umbra asked Rupert for the story, and Rupert told him about the betrayal during the Civil War.

By the time he had finished, encouraged by questions from Madeline, Umbra, and even Morpeth, the meal was over. As the ladies stood, so did the gentlemen, Rupert a beat behind. He realised, almost too late, that allowing the ladies to withdraw would leave Madeline alone with the Ice Dragon.

"Lady Penworth, Lady Wyvern, given we are so few at table, may I beg your indulgence for the gentlemen to join you immediately?" he said.

Morpeth gave another patronising chuckle. "The newlyweds cannot bear to be parted, it seems."

In the blue drawing room, Lady Wyvern presided over the tea tray. The men all refused a cup, instead, accepting a port from the decanter Graviton carried from the dining room. Madeline took her own fragrant cup of Oolong to a seat beside Rupert, and listened as Morpeth began a searching interrogation about affairs of state. Rupert, veteran of thousands of such discussions with his tutors and Lord Wyvern, was only too happy, and soon was eagerly questioning Morpeth about the progress of the war, the impact of the death of William Pitt, and the policies of Grenville, the new Prime Minister. Umbra was drawn in when Morpeth referred several questions to him, and then, Graviton and Lady Wyvern. Madeline—who had her knowledge of such matters from newspapers and books—listened, enthralled, as the other five talked about people whose decisions shaped the world she knew.

"But we are boring Lady Penworth," said Morpeth, after a while. "You would rather hear about the latest fashions, I have no doubt, my dear," he told her, smiling indulgently.

"I am finding it interesting, my lord," Madeline told him. "And I will need to know such things to be the countess my husband needs, will I not?"

"No, no, I know what you young ladies like. You will want to know that the sleeves in evening gowns this autumn are quite full, and square necks are quite the rage. I daresay you should be surprised, Lady Penworth, at the length some ladies wear their dusters—why, I have seen a train of several feet! One has to be most careful where one steps. When you go up to London, you shall…"

Morpeth continued for several minutes, seeking support for his comments and opinions from Lady Wyvern, who soon looked nearly as impatient as Madeline felt. "But now we are boring the gentlemen," Lady Wyvern said. "Penworth, perhaps you and your wife would favour us with some music. I had Morris bring your violin."

Sure enough, the familiar case was on the pianoforte in the corner of the room. Madeline squeezed Rupert's hand. He did not allow the servants to touch even the case of his precious Lady, and would be deeply indignant about Lady Wyvern's presumption. But, though his face was white and mouth pinched, he managed to control whatever protest welled behind his gritted teeth.

Madeline stood, and he came with her, gripping her hand until it hurt.

She had not practiced on a pianoforte for months, though she played the spinet daily. She preferred the richer, more complex sound of the pianoforte, but would her fingers remember what was required of them? She had no doubt Rupert would adapt and make them both sound good.

Rupert checked his violin, calming as he did so, while Madeline looked through the folder of music that had also been retrieved by some intruder into their tower sanctuary. She took a deep breath. Calm. She, too, needed to be calm.

A low-voiced consultation on which piece to play and they began, soon losing themselves in the joy of handing the music back and forth, supporting one another, making something beautiful together that was greater than either could create apart.

Morpeth had tears in his eyes when Madeline looked up after the final notes died into silence. "That was beautiful, my lord, my lady. Beautiful. May I prevail upon you…?"

"Perhaps tomorrow evening, Morpeth, if you would be kind enough to allow us to take our leave." Rupert told him.

"Thank you for your kindness, Lord Morpeth, but I am sure the company will understand I need my sleep." Madeline coloured, but her implication had the desired result, Lord Morpeth assuring her he understood entirely, and his own dear wife was much the same when she was… "Ahem."

Lady Wyvern's lips thinned, but she made no motion to stop their progress to the door, so Madeline was unsurprised to find Morris and several sturdy footmen waiting in the hall immediately outside. Rupert ignored them, turning towards the tower with his violin case in one hand and Madeline's hand in the other, walking so fast Madeline had to hurry to keep up.

The escort left them at the door, and Rupert sent Morris and Polly away, too. "My wife and I will serve one another," he said, too firmly to permit argument.

As they prepared for bed, and while lying in one another's arms, they pooled their impressions of Morpeth and his secretary. Was it good or bad for them that Morpeth seemed willing to be convinced Rupert was both capable and sane?

Madeline drifted into sleep, praying they would have an opportunity on the morrow to speak to one or both men alone.

Six

They spent an anxious morning trying to follow their normal routine, then two stout footmen arrived with a message from Lady Wyvern, commanding Rupert's presence, and he reluctantly left Madeline and allowed himself to be escorted down to the castle's library.

"Ah, Penworth. Graviton has been showing me the earldom's ledgers. Very impressive. Very impressive. You placed your trust in the right man in Graviton." Lord Morpeth clapped Rupert on his shoulder, and Rupert swallowed to ease the rigid muscles of his jaw.

"I have been pleased to be able to give my sister and her husband a few months of leisure," Graviton demurred. "Lord Wyvern wanted it so, of course, but with his illness..." Graviton let the words trail off.

"Shall I read out loud the passages you wanted His Lordship's comment on, Lord Morpeth?" That was the secretary.

Rupert rather enjoyed the next hour. Anything Morpeth asked that related to the business of the earldom before his incarceration, he answered with ease. And he took pleasure in grilling Graviton when the questions turned to more recent activities and events. He had to concede, however reluctantly, that Graviton had done a fair job as steward of the estates, just as Morpeth had indicated. Which was all to the good, of course. He would not wish his people to suffer. But it irked him, nonetheless, to find a virtue in the man.

Finally, Lord Morpeth pronounced himself satisfied, and suggested they join the ladies.

Rupert knew Madeline was in the drawing room as soon as he entered, before she crossed the room to tuck her hand under his elbow.

"Are you well, Wife?" he asked. *Has my sister hurt you or threatened you*, he wanted to know, but she seemed calm.

"I am," she assured him. "And you?"

"Well," he confirmed. "I have been going over our books with Lord Morpeth. Your brother has done a good job while we have been here, but it is time we ran our own estates, my lady."

Graviton sounded smug. "It has been my pleasure, Penworth. And I'll continue happily for a while yet. You need not concern yourself, I assure you."

"How delightful," Lord Morpeth said, "to see such amity. It is not always so at Court. Now, Lady Wyvern, once I have seen Lord Wyvern, I believe our business will be concluded. I shall be taking good reports back to the King, you may be certain."

"I am just awaiting word that Lord Wyvern is awake and able to meet with visitors," Lady Wyvern said.

Madeline grasped Rupert's arm, silently offering her support, and he covered her hand with his own. "I, too, am anxious to see Lord Wyvern," he said, and was pleased at how calm and even his voice sounded.

"You shall see him shortly, Penworth." Lady Wyvern said shortly, and her lover broke in, explaining to Morpeth, "When Lord Wyvern took an ague, His Lordship thought it best not to visit, lest he put my sister and the babe at risk. It must be… why, two weeks since he last saw his father's old friend. Is that not right, Penworth?"

"It feels like six months," Rupert replied, and Madeline squeezed his arm again, as Graviton turned the remark off. "The impatience of youth. Of course, Lord Wyvern has been a father to him these last ten years."

"Indeed." Lady Wyvern agreed. "I feel more his mother than his sister." Her voice suspiciously maudlin, she added, "His own dear mother was my closest friend when we were young together. Did I not love him for our father's sake and my own, I must love him for the sake of poor, lost Emmaline…"

Lord Morpeth gave a deep sigh.

"How charming, my lady. You and the former countess made your debut together, did you not?"

Rupert had pieced together the story from servants' gossip and his sister's occasional vituperative remarks: two reigning beauties, rivals rather than friends, one an earl's daughter and the other, the only child of a viscount. At the end of the season, the viscount's daughter was married to the earl, while her rival was the centre of an unspoken scandal, saved from complete disgrace by marriage to her father's closest friend.

"We did, Lord Morpeth," Lady Wyvern agreed.

"The toasts of London, or so I hear, though I cannot believe, my lady, it was long enough ago for your friend's son to be a grown man. Why, you look scarcely older than Her Ladyship, here."

"And the two friends became sisters," Madeline cooed. "How sweet." If anyone else caught the sarcastic edge to her voice, they did not remark on it, but it cheered Rupert. The Ice Dragon and her lover could force their compliance, but could not divide them.

"Ah," said Graviton. "Here is the nurse. Your patient is ready, Miss Tyler?"

The nurse must have given some nonverbal signal, because Lady Wyvern said, "Come, Lord Morpeth. You and I shall lead the way."

The nurse reeked of the sickroom—an odour Rupert remembered from his own convalescence. Sweat was part of it, and dust. His nostrils flared at the sickly stench of opium. Was Lord Wyvern in such pain, then? Under it all, he could detect perfumes that must be the nurse's own, from her soap or perhaps her clothes. Rosemary, and some more floral note; carnation, perhaps.

Their procession led to the tower across the courtyard from Rupert's and Madeline's.

"We have moved him to an upper room, Lord Morpeth," Lady Wyvern was saying. "The doctor assures us it is for the best. The breezes at this height will carry away the noxious odours that cause disease."

But when they came into the tower room, which smelt almost airy and fresh, if one ignored the undercurrents of opium and illness, Lady Wyvern turned on the nurse. "Close the windows and curtains, woman. Do you wish to kill His Lordship?"

"The breezes will keep the room fresh," the nurse replied, calmly. Her voice, thin and quavering, sounded old, which surprised Rupert, who had thought her young by her smell.

The voice from the bed drove everything else out of Rupert's head. "Rupert, my boy," he thought Lord Wyvern had tried to say, though his voice was slurred and rusty with disuse. Rupert crossed the room, barely conscious of his wife guiding him around obstacles, to kneel at his mentor's side and cover his hand with kisses and tears. Until this moment, he had not allowed himself to either hope or grieve.

"You p-p-omized." Lord Wyvern was stern, and Rupert winced. He had broken many promises by allowing himself to be imprisoned. But Lady Wyvern answered, "Yes, my lord. I promised that you should see Penworth today, and here he is. And you shall have many more visits with him, dear husband, if you but take care not to over-exert yourself or bother your head about business, which you can safely leave to me and to Sir James Graviton, here."

The hand Rupert held jerked convulsively. "Keep… boy… safe."

"Yes, you can see for yourself Penworth is perfectly safe, and will, we devoutly pray, remain so." Lady Wyvern's voice was soothing, and Rupert doubted Morpeth could hear the smug message underlying her words.

"Now, Wyvern, Lord Morpeth has a few questions, and then tomorrow—if all goes well—you shall have a short visit with Penworth and his little wife."

"Just two questions, Wyvern," Morpeth said, his voice hushed and gentle, as if he spoke to a child rather than an invalid. "I would not ask, but—duty to the King, you know."

Lord Wyvern made a noise Morpeth must have interpreted as consent. "Would you say Rupert Fleming, Earl of Penworth, is capable of undertaking the duties of his high office?"

Wyvern made the same noise, and Morpeth nodded, smiling. "Yes, I think so, too. A very able young man. And now, my dear sir, will you confirm Penworth married with your consent? I have seen the marriage licence, you understand, signed by the bride and groom, but Penworth was still a minor. I must be able to assure the king the marriage is valid."

Lord Wyvern's hand convulsed in Rupert's, and Rupert felt Madeline come up behind him and rest her hand on his shoulder. What would Lord Wyvern say? How could Rupert convey to his old mentor how much Madeline meant to him? If Lord Wyvern repudiated the marriage, Rupert would simply marry Madeline again, but surely, Lord Morpeth would repeat such a juicy piece of scandal the length and breadth of the *ton*, which would embarrass her. Somehow, he and Madeline would get out of their current predicament, and he wanted his wife to be comfortable in London society.

What could he say?

"Sir," he said, "although, when this marriage was first suggested, I was reluctant, I could not be better pleased with my dear wife. She is my cherished companion and partner, and will soon be the mother of my child."

Lord Wyvern's hand convulsed again, then he made the same affirmative noise as before.

"Excellent," Lord Morpeth said. "Excellent. Wyvern, my dear fellow, we must let you rest. I see your good nurse glaring at me from the shadows."

Lord Wyvern clung to Rupert's hand, letting go only reluctantly when Lady Wyvern repeated that they would be allowed a visit tomorrow.

Back down in the courtyard, she turned to Morpeth, saying, "You will be anxious to leave, Lord Morpeth. The next boat sails with the tide at three of the clock."

Lord Morpeth was cheerfully unconcerned. "One more night makes little difference, Lady Wyvern."

"It is unlikely to be just the one night," Graviton offered.

"Unfortunately, Sir James is correct," Lady Wyvern agreed. "The weather is expected to close in tomorrow, and our boats may be stuck in the harbour here until the storm passes."

"My wife and I will farewell you from the dock," Rupert said. Perhaps he would have a chance to talk to Morpeth or his secretary alone, or—at worst—perhaps they could simply jump onto the boat as it pulled away from the dock.

"No, Penworth. I am confident Lord Morpeth will not wish to take up any more of the time you and the countess have together. Your duties will come between you soon enough. Say goodbye to His Lordship now, if you please." Though she tried to make it sound like a suggestion, still, it was a command.

Well then. This was his only chance. He could trade his own safety and the survival of his violin for the safety of his wife, and stated in those terms the decision was easy.

"Take the countess with you, Lord Morpeth, I beg you. She is not safe here. Lady Wyvern and Graviton have been keeping us prisoner, and they mean her harm."

Lady Wyvern tried to brush it off. "Such a joke is in poor taste, Penworth."

"I beg you, Lord Morpeth," Rupert repeated. Madeline had both her hands on his arm now, and he covered them with his free hand to calm their shaking.

"Alas," Graviton said mournfully, "Louisa, I fear his illness has returned. He has spells, Morpeth, but he has been so well since his marriage…"

"The blow to his head, you know, in the accident that killed my brother," Lady Wyvern explained. "The last two days have been too much for him, I fear."

"I am not sure…" Morpeth began.

"Sir, you have examined me. You know I am sane."

The secretary interrupted, "Lord Morpeth, we must be on our way, or we shall miss the tide. I am certain Lady Wyvern will take good care of her brother."

"No," Morpeth declared. "I know my duty. We will have to stay, Umbra. I must investigate these charges."

"What a nuisance," Lady Wyvern sighed. She must have made some signal, for immediately he heard scuffling, and hands seized his shoulders and arms. Madeline was clinging hard, but being pulled away.

"Be careful with the countess, you fools," Lady Wyvern commanded. "She is carrying the future Penworth!"

"Rupert!" Madeline screamed his name as her fingers were pried from his arm and she was carried away. He reached out for her. "Madeline! Madeline!"

"Rupert!" Her voice calling his name echoed in his mind long after the sound faded, as he was hustled along in a phalanx of hard-handed men, across the courtyard and down a flight of stairs into the oldest part of the castle. Then more stairs. The dungeons. Of course.

He was hurled down into what he knew to be the first of a series of cells and had not picked himself up from the floor before first one man, and then another, cannonaded down after him. Morpeth and Umbra, by the shape and odour, and they confirmed it immediately, Morpeth cursing vigorously and Umbra apologising, as he lifted himself off the pair of them.

From the top of the stairs, Lady Wyvern spoke. "You fool, Penworth. What did you hope to achieve with your dramatics? Now you have written a death warrant for our visitors, and for yourself, unless the child is a daughter."

"You treacherous bitch," Morpeth spluttered, but Lady Wyvern just laughed, a sound cut off by the slamming door, the bolts outside screeching as they were shot home.

"That could have gone better," Umbra said quietly. He was fumbling about, and Rupert heard a repeated tapping, and then some soft, huffing breaths.

"Thank God," Morpeth breathed devoutly. "Light."

"The room has been used recently," Umbra said. "By an invalid, I would say. Lord Wyvern, perhaps?"

"Surely not," Morpeth objected. "We saw his room!"

"He was moved there this past week," Rupert observed. "My wife watched it from the window."

He was prowling the room, confirming his childhood memories of its size and dimensions. This was the cell purported to contain the ghost, and so, had been of unending fascination to his younger self.

Morpeth was still objecting. "Lord Wyvern was not himself, but surely, if he had been kept here, he would have made a complaint!"

"Lord Wyvern was drugged. At a guess, I would say with opium," Umbra informed his master. "And undoubtedly, Lady Wyvern and Graviton threatened harm to Lord Penworth if Lord Wyvern tried to alert you to their plotting."

"Such wickedness! Her own husband!"

"And her own brother," Rupert reminded the man. "And his own sister."

"Indeed. Indeed. Umbra, you see how wrong you were to insist we leave."

"To be fair, Lord Morpeth, it was probably too late by then. But had you said nothing, Lord Penworth, and had we been allowed to leave when I suggested it, we could be organising a rescue by now. You were not to know that, of course, my lord."

"You knew we were prisoners here?"

"I suspected it," Umbra confirmed, "and when I saw Lord Wyvern's condition, I was certain."

"Tell me," Rupert commanded. "He has lost weight. I could feel how thin his hand was. And his voice… so frail, and so hard to understand. He is very ill? Is he… is he dying, Umbra?"

"I do not know, Sir. We will need to get him away from that pair. We can trust his nurse to do what she can for him, but I cannot give you any assurance his condition will improve without knowing what is wrong."

"Never mind Wyvern," Morpeth burst out. "What about us? You heard Lady Wyvern. They intend to kill us!"

Seven

Madeline, locked back in the tower, took refuge in a hearty bout of tears. It was, in part, genuine; she could not help but worry about Rupert, though she thought—she hoped—the Ice Dragon and her lover would not hurt him till they were sure of the baby. Mostly, though, she wept to confound her jailers.

Madeline thought Polly would probably support her, left to herself, but Morris was Lady Wyvern's man through and through. He must be led to believe Madeline was defeated. She could do nothing until after dark, in any case, and it was pleasing to hear

Polly fretting to Morris about the possible impact of her grief on the health of the child she carried.

In the end, Polly left and came back with Graviton, who was at first impatient, and then inclined to be worried. As Madeline had hoped, he was reluctant to use force on her, and harsh words only made her cry harder. In the end, he resorted to bribery and threats.

"Nothing will happen to your earl as long as you behave, Mad. If you keep weeping like this and harm the baby, why, we'll have to hurt him in some way. Some way that won't prevent him from making another. We could cut off a finger, perhaps. Oh, hush that noise, you fool. We won't hurt him if you are good."

Madeline allowed her wails to subside to smothered sobs, with the occasional great, shuddering gasp, for effect.

"There, that's better. Now, let Polly here put you to bed."

"But I need my husband," Madeline wailed. "I cannot sleep without my husband."

Graviton was looking decidedly hunted. "Louisa won't allow it, Mad. But perhaps I can talk her 'round. Just give me some time."

Madeline did her best to look grateful. "P-p-please? I will try not to cry. But it is so h-h-hard."

"If you stop crying, I will talk to Louisa," he agreed. "It won't be immediately, mind. But if you are good, and the earl is good... Yes, I think we can manage something."

Madeline nodded and blinked rapidly, so the tears in her eyes spilled down her cheeks.

"I will try," she said again. "Thank you, Graviton."

He left, and Madeline allowed herself to be washed and changed for bed, responding dully and without interest to Polly's ministrations. After the maid had tucked her into bed and asked for the fourth time if, "Your Ladyship wants anything at all," she finally left, whispering as she departed, "I am certain there will be good news in the morning, my lady."

Madeline was out of bed as soon as Polly was out the door, and from the top of the stair, she heard the maid talking to whomever let her out of the tower. "I don't feel right about leaving my poor countess alone, and that's the truth."

"We heard her," one of the guards commented. "Thought it was the White Lady!"

"Poor dearling," Polly said. "She is that grieved! It is wicked, separating her from the earl. Just wicked. But she will not have me stay by her…"

The voice faded as the door shut, and Madeline hastened back to her dressing room to change into something that would allow her to climb. A pair of Rupert's knee breeches, in the darkest colour she could find, with a morning gown over the top. It fastened at the front, so she could button herself up. She tucked the gown into the breeches and slipped on a pair of soft shoes that would give her a good grip. A shawl, in case it was cold? Lady Wyvern had said a storm was coming.

Next, she hurried upstairs to fetch three great skeins of knitted ladder from their various hiding places, fumbling for them in the gloom—she would not risk attracting attention with a light. The darkness meant she could not see Rupert's violin. How she wished she could take it with her! But Rupert and the baby must come first.

Back down to the lowest level of the prison where she had been so happy these past months. It was the work of minutes to firmly tie the three pieces to form one long ladder, and then to fasten the two long arms of the top piece around the largest, heaviest piece of furniture in the room: a grotesque armoire that must have been built in place, since it could never have been carried up the winding tower stair or hoisted through the narrow window.

She leant out the window. She could see no movement in the courtyard below, nothing in the tower opposite or any of the other rooms that overlooked the courtyard.

Climbing down was harder than she expected. The ladder blew in the wind, and every rung had to be felt for, then turned, so she could put her foot firmly in place. As soon as she had her weight on a knitted rung, it would stretch, pulling the sides closer together, so she could not put the other foot beside the first, but needed to either dangle, gathering her strength, or reach further down for the next rung. Her weight also pulled her against the rough stone of the tower, bruising and grazing her knuckles and toes, even through her gloves and slippers.

She kept going, one rung at a time, refusing to be discouraged, refusing to think about how far she had come or how far she could fall.

Then, all at once, it was over. Her foot stretched and touched the cobblestones of the courtyard, and just like that, the climb was done.

As soon as she took her weight from the ladder, the wind whipped it into the air, and she imagined it streaming out from the tower window far above her head. Hidden in the shadows, she let her gown back down around her feet.

Several minutes passed, and all remained quiet. This might actually work! First, she needed to find a boat small enough for her to handle. Hugging the walls, keeping to the shadows, she began to circle the courtyard toward the deeper darkness that signalled the passageway through the walls. Beyond, the road led down to the docks.

She was nearly there when a woman's voice spoke behind her. "Do not be alarmed, Lady Penworth."

Madeline spun around, one hand to her chest to hold her pounding heart in place.

"Who is it?" She could see a vague shape in the darkness, but no details.

"A friend."

It was not Lady Wyvern, nor—from the accent, which was aristocratic—one of the servants. As she froze, trying to decide whether to run or speak, she heard footsteps and voices approaching from the other end of the passage.

"Quick. This way." The woman took her hand and pulled her through a doorway, into the room beyond. Just in time. Pressed against the wall inside the door, she could hear them clearly: several men arguing in hushed voices.

"It was the White Lady, I tell you."

"Rubbish."

"She was coming out that window. I saw her with my own eyes. It was like a long coil of smoke, twisting in the wind."

"A long coil of smoke. Listen to him. Next, you'll be telling us she's off to join her husband in the dungeon."

A chorus of guffaws.

"You've heard what the islanders say, same as me," the first voice insisted.

"Yes, and right fools they are, too." The speaker pitched his voice in a falsetto. "Ooooh! Moaning in the dungeon. It must be the ghost!" Then, reverting to his own low rumble. "Silly tossers. A good thing Her Ladyship sent the whole lot of them packing."

The first voice began, "If you ask me…"

Another man interrupted. "You can stand around talking about ghosts all night if you want. I'm for the kitchen and a tot of something hot and strong. Securing those boats was cold work."

She could make out no more. They were across the courtyard and… yes, they had gone down the steps into the servants' area Rupert had pointed out from their window.

"Come," her companion said. "Lord Wyvern is awake and wishes to speak with you."

"Let me go," Madeline pleaded. "Now, while the courtyard is clear."

"I will help you, my lady. That is why I am here. But first, we need to share information. Come with me and see Lord Wyvern."

"Who are you?" Madeline asked, but the woman gave her no answer, just moved away, surefooted in the dark.

After a moment, Madeline followed her. They climbed the stair until they reached the room where Lord Wyvern lay, propped up on pillows, looking—by the light of the lamp at his bedside—more alert than he had earlier in the day.

The light allowed Madeline to recognise her companion. "You are the nurse. Miss Tyler. You work for Lady Wyvern."

"I work for Lord Wyvern," Miss Tyler corrected. "I am here to rescue him, and you and the earl."

"Lady Wyvern took the earl away. I don't know where."

"Dun… jin," Lord Wyvern said, and Miss Tyler nodded. "They were keeping Lord Wyvern in the dungeon when I was brought here to care for him. I expect that is where they have your husband and the other two men."

Lord Wyvern was a frail shadow of the hearty man Rupert had described, and pale enough to have been in a dungeon these six months. Madeline didn't understand how his own servants could have allowed such a thing.

"Why did your people let it happen?" she asked him, but it was Miss Tyler who answered.

"His Lordship had an apoplexy. Lady Wyvern saw her moment and removed anyone who might object to her regency while he was ill. Then, when he began to recover… well, she made sure to keep him bedridden. And she hid him, so those loyal to him would not know what she was doing."

"How could the Ice Dragon hope to get away with it?"

Goodness. She was so used to Rupert's name for his sister that she said it without thinking. But Lord Wyvern was laughing silently, and even the nurse was smiling.

"A good name for her," Miss Tyler said. "She is an arrogant woman, Your Ladyship. She makes her plans and assumes the rest of the world will fall into line. She must have been horrified when the King sent Lord Morpeth to see what was happening here, but she and Sir James decided to bully their way through.

"They sent most of the islanders away, to keep complaints and rumours from reaching Lord Morpeth's ears. That may yet work to her disadvantage, since they are now on the mainland and will be talking to all their friends and relatives. Word will reach the ears of the gentry sooner or later, and people with authority will start asking questions."

"I cannot wait for that," Madeline said. "I need to rescue the earl now."

"Plan?" Lord Wyvern asked.

"Yes, my lady. What was your plan? Do you have a helper? Somewhere to go?"

Madeline shook her head. She and Rupert had no one to help them. But they had a plan, of sorts, and she intended to carry it out.

Miss Tyler saw her hesitation. "Lady Penworth, you are wise to be cautious, but you can trust us. Lord Wyvern, as you know, is as much a victim of the conspirators as you and your husband. And I have been sent by the earl's godmother to find out what is happening and help if I can."

"How did you come to be His Lordship's nurse?" Madeline asked. Perhaps the woman's explanation would suggest how to proceed.

"Pure chance. I travelled on the same coach as the woman they had sent to nurse Lord Wyvern into sufficient health to meet the King's man. And when I found out where she was going, and the job for which she had been hired, I persuaded her to let me take her place."

Madeline looked at Lord Wyvern in some consternation. If this were his improved condition, how sick had he been?

"Go-w-d," he said.

"Yes," Miss Tyler agreed. "Gold. I paid her double the fee she had been promised and sent her back to London, to my employer."

Madeline made up her mind. In truth, she had been worried about how she would manage without another pair of hands.

"I was heading for the harbour," she said, "to the boats."

"No!" Lord Wyvern tried to sit up, but failed. "Storm!"

Madeline put a hand on his to reassure him. "Just to let a boat go, Lord Wyvern, so they think I have escaped that way. Not to actually set sail."

"Very clever." The nurse nodded. "And then hide while they chase after you, yes?"

"That was what we planned. But now I need to find Rupert."

"Tide," Lord Wyvern insisted. "Wait for tide. Tide take boat out."

The two women exchanged glances. "Do you know what time that will be, my lord?" Miss Tyler asked.

"I do." Madeline remembered the exchange with Lord Morpeth. "Today's tide was ebbing at three of the clock, so will it not ebb again around the same time in the night?"

"A little later, perhaps, but yes. That is good. We shall let the boat drift out to sea on the tide." Miss Tyler checked a timepiece that lay near the lamp. "We have two hours to wait. Shall we see if we can find the gentlemen?"

She turned to Lord Wyvern. "Let me see to your comfort before we go, my lord, and we shall return as soon as we can."

Lord Wyvern shook his head. "No. Leave me. She find you here."

Miss Tyler frowned.

"Yes!" Lord Wyvern insisted. "Get earl safe. Wife, too. Come back later."

Was his speech growing clearer, or was Madeline just becoming used to it?

"Rupert will not leave you, my lord," she assured him.

"Get later," he commanded. "Tell Rupe… Tunn'ls. Go through tunn'ls. Boy knows."

Miss Tyler's quick mind leapt ahead. "Another way out of the dungeons, my lord?"

Lord Wyvern nodded. Yes.

They discussed their options as they helped Lord Wyvern to a drink, and then to relieve himself. (Madeline blushed and looked away, but Miss Tyler seemed untroubled.) Miss Tyler settled him on his pillows and gave him a carefully measured spoonful of medicine from a bottle that stood ready.

His eyes asked a question, and she said, "The diluted version, my lord. We shall taper you off, never you fear. And I have in mind a use for the extra we have saved." She took another, almost identical, bottle and secreted it somewhere about her person. "Come, my lady. Fare thee well, my lord. I shall return as soon as I can."

Madeline stopped to kiss Lord Wyvern's papery cheek, for Rupert's sake, then followed Miss Tyler out of the room and down out of the tower.

The courtyard was empty, nothing moving except a few weeds tossing in the wind in neglected corners.

Miss Tyler led the way to the steps into the service area, where the party from the harbour had entered not long before. "This is the quickest way," she whispered.

The door let onto a narrow passage with several doorways on either side, some dark and some lit. "Keep your shawl over your head, my lady, and be ready to duck out of sight," Miss Tyler advised at a whisper.

But no one emerged from the kitchen, where they could hear conversation and laughter, nor from any of the other rooms. Miss Tyler led Madeline to a door near the end of the passage. "We need to go through here, but I have an idea to deal with the guards. Wait out of sight. I won't be a moment."

When she returned, several minutes later, it was with another servant, who courteously opened the outside door for her, since her hands were occupied with a tray containing a tankard and a plate of bread and cheese. Madeline shrank back into the shadows, hiding her face with the edge of her dark shawl, but the servant returned to the kitchen without looking her way.

The outside door reopened, and Miss Tyler returned, putting the tray on the sideboard at one side of the hall. Madeline joined her as Miss Tyler retrieved two smaller tankards from the shelf above, poured into each half the contents of the bottle she'd brought from

Lord Wyvern's sick room, and topped them up from the larger tankard she had fetched in the kitchen.

Madeline watched with admiration as Miss Tyler then transformed herself into a maid, washing her face to remove the lines that had given her the appearance of age, hiding her hair under a mob cap she pulled from a hidden pocket, and fetching a tablecloth from within the sideboard to tie around her waist as an apron.

"In the kitchen, they are nervous," she told Madeline as she worked her metamorphosis. "They have gone along with your imprisonment, but most of them did not know about Lord Wyvern, and they are unhappy with what they've heard of his treatment. Casting the King's man into the dungeon has them running scared. Several are nearly ready to flee, or even turn on Lady Wyvern and your brother."

She picked up the tray. "I will take their refreshments to the guards in the dungeon," she told Madeline. "Follow me, but stay back, so they don't see you."

"Can I not be a maid, too?" Madeline asked.

"Not in a silk gown, Your Ladyship." Miss Tyler went to pick up the tray, then stopped. "Can you shoot a pistol, by any chance?"

Madeline nodded, and from that same mysterious source Miss Tyler produced a small gun with a chased design in silver and a carved wooden handle, and a pouch of ammunition to load in it. Quickly, Miss Tyler unscrewed the barrel and poured black powder into the chamber. She added a bullet and replaced the barrel.

"Do not shoot unless we are threatened. I would prefer the guards have their supper and go peacefully to sleep. It will be quieter and less messy. But if they attempt to raise the alarm, I will need you to silence one while I deal with the other." She frowned slightly, examining Madeline. "Can you do it? Can you shoot someone, Lady Penworth? I will not think less of you for being honest, if you cannot."

"I can shoot any person that threatens harm to my husband, Miss Tyler," Madeline said, hoping it were true. She had learned to use firearms so she could train her dogs not to be afraid of the noise, but she had only ever fired at targets. Her throat tightened at the thought of shooting a human being. But she must have sounded convincing, because Miss Tyler nodded, collected the tray, and led the way to the dungeon stairs.

Eight

Morpeth was fretting, and had been doing so for hours. Rupert wished he would stop, or at least fret in silence. Instead, he repeated a litany, always the same, starting with the excuses he should have given the King, passing through all the things he should have noticed (or that Umbra should have pointed out to him), and ending with speculations about the time and manner of his death, before beginning again with the excuses.

Umbra, who remained unaccountably cheerful, ignored him after the first round, and recommended Rupert do likewise. But Rupert was afraid that several hours in a dungeon with Morpeth would achieve what the weeks alone before his wedding could not: drive him mad.

He resorted to imagining the fingering and bow movements for the concerto he and Madeline were currently learning. Deep inside his own thoughts, rehearsing a particularly tricky passage, a sound outside caught his attention.

"Quiet." The peremptory order stopped Morpeth mid-complaint. Rupert sank to his knees beside the door, pressing his ear against it. It had been made from one massive piece of oak, but over the years, it had dried and twisted slightly, leaving a sliver of gap between door and frame where sound from without carried more or less clearly, at least to ears as acute as Rupert's.

In some part of his brain, he registered Morpeth asking questions and Umbra silencing him in a manner nearly as abrupt as Rupert's. All Rupert's attention was on the conversation outside.

"Miss Tyler?" he asked no one in particular. "What is she doing here?"

"Good girl!" Umbra remarked, unsurprised.

"She is giving the guards something to eat and drink," Rupert reported. "They are being lewd. I hope she knows what she is about."

"Trust her for that," Umbra said, but with an undertone of concern that suggested he was not as confident as he wished Rupert to think.

But the guards' crass remarks were already becoming more slurred, less forceful, and they soon ceased entirely, replaced by snoring that was crass in quite a different fashion.

"I think she has given them something to make them sleep," Rupert said.

"Probably some of Lord Wyvern's opium." Umbra suggested.

"You expected this?" Morpeth was inclined to be indignant.

"I expected Miss T would do something. I did not know what."

Rupert was still listening. "Miss Tyler is talking to someone. I cannot hear the reply, but she does not sound distressed."

In the next moment, he straightened, beaming. "It is my wife!"

They all heard the key turn in the lock, and Madeline was first through the door when it opened, walking into Rupert's waiting arms, clutching him as if they had been separated for weeks, rather than hours.

"Madeline," he murmured into her hair.

"If you would move out of the doorway, my lord, my lady…"

Rupert shifted sideways at Miss Tyler's voice, but did not let go of his wife, nor she of him, ignoring the movements of the others in and out of the cell, until her presence in his arms eased the hard knot of tension of which he had not even been aware.

"Would you give the gun to Umbra now, please, countess?" Miss Tyler asked. Ah. That must be the hard object his wife was holding clutched in the hand pressed into his back. It disappeared.

"A gun, Madeline?" Rupert asked.

"I am glad I did not have to shoot it," Madeline confided. "I learned to fire a gun to train the dogs, but I have never killed anything."

"You did very well, my lady," Miss Tyler said. "Lady Penworth climbed from the tower on a ladder she had knitted, Umbra."

"It worked? Well done, Madeline." Rupert clutched her still closer at the thought of her dangling, precariously, sixty yards above the hard stones of the courtyard. He had always intended to go first, and had imagined a dozen different ways to make it unnecessary for her to try it at all. But it had worked, and she was here, and his foolish heart did not need to pound as if she were broken at the foot of the tower.

"I wish I could have released the ladder when I was down," Madeline said. "The Ice Dragon will know how I escaped."

"Yes, it is a pity. Perhaps..." Miss Tyler did not finish that sentence, but instead went on, in a brisker voice. "We need to complete this escape before we do anything else. Lord Penworth, Lord Wyvern suggested you lead us out of here through the smugglers' tunnel. I suggest we then release the boat, as you and the countess had planned, and take refuge in the tower with Lord Wyvern."

"A smugglers' tunnel, eh? That gives me an idea." Umbra sounded as if he were grinning. "Confusion is an excellent thing in one's enemy, do you not agree, Morpeth?"

"What have you in mind?" Miss Tyler asked.

"Put the candle back in the cell, and I shall lock the door and return the key to the guards. Let them puzzle out how we managed to walk through solid walls!"

Miss Tyler grinned. "Perfect. The guards are unlikely to admit they fell asleep on the job, and the one who should be at the door, but is instead toasting his toes at the kitchen fire, will assure Lady Wyvern no one passed him by. And he will be right."

"But we cannot go into these tunnels without a light," Morpeth objected.

"Lord Penworth does not need a light." From the sounds, Umbra was suiting action to words. "There. Done. Lead on, Lord Penworth."

Rupert had not been in the tunnels for years, but the key was simple enough. One left, two right, two left, one right, and repeat— and a cross symbol cut into the lintel of each correct tunnel. He had grown since the old days of exploration. He no longer needed to stretch to reach the confirming sign.

They walked in a chain: Madeline holding his hand, then Morpeth, Miss Tyler, and Umbra bringing up the rear. Morpeth had stopped complaining after the second command from Umbra to keep quiet, lest echoes travel up through the complex of caves and alert someone in the castle.

Morpeth and Umbra were sounding less and less like master and secretary. Who was Umbra, really? Lord Wyvern had told Rupert of men who served the Crown in various guises, giving up their own identities—and the virtue of honesty—for the sake of the nation. Was Umbra one of those? Was Miss Tyler? He had never imagined women as spies, but how useful to be a spy nobody would imagine!

There. If he remembered correctly, this was the last tunnel. One long curve would bring them into the back of a cave, with a single right-angled turn to the shore.

Sure enough, moments later, those behind him commented on the light. "Relative light," Umbra corrected. "It is only light by comparison with the cave. Well done, my lord."

"Thank God," Morpeth breathed. "Now, how do we get off this island?"

"First, let us see what we can do to confound pursuit," Miss Tyler suggested. "Umbra, Lord and Lady Penworth intended to set a boat adrift to confuse the trail. Would you and Lord Morpeth do that? And I shall see if I can remove Lady Penworth's ladder."

"Morpeth and I can deal with the boats, Miss T, but how will you get into the tower?" Umbra asked.

"The guards were about to perform the changeover when I was in the kitchen, and the man who is there now was most vocal about the danger of killing a noble, and a King's emissary at that. I think he will take little persuasion to let me in, and to let me out again once I've dealt with the ladder."

"What of us?" Rupert asked.

"Would you and the countess wait here, my lord? You can retreat into the tunnels if someone comes searching, and Lady Penworth and the baby will be safe."

"I do not like sending you to do the work while I hide," Rupert said.

"Nor is it wise," Madeline pointed out, "to leave Lord Wyvern vulnerable."

Umbra was quick to see the point. "Lady Wyvern could use him to make us surrender. One of us needs to defend his tower."

"Give me the gun," Madeline suggested, "and the earl and I shall go. We shall barricade ourselves in the tower with Lord Wyvern and come to no harm."

"A blind man, a woman, and a bedridden invalid?" Morpeth said. "It sounds like a disaster in the making."

"It sounds sensible to me," Umbra countered. "If they barricade themselves in, only an axe will get them out. And any assailants will have to come up the stairs one at a time. Lady Penworth, you said you use guns in your dog training. Do you know how to load this one?"

"Yes," Madeline said.

Umbra handed her the gun, and Miss Tyler gave her the pouch of ammunition and powder, saying, "We will come as quickly as we can, and if we cannot reach you, one of us will go to the mainland for help. Hold out, and this will all be settled today."

Umbra and Lord Morpeth went around the rocks towards the harbour, feeling their way in the dark. The others took the narrow path up from the small beach to the castle, Rupert leading the way, the two women close behind.

He stopped just below the main path down to the harbour.

"What is wrong?" Miss Tyler asked.

Rupert shushed her. Some people were coming down the path, arguing in hushed voices. In moments, they were close enough to make out the words.

"I tell 'ee, we should stay and demand our pay," said one.

"Demand? From Her Ladyship? You'd get paid in bullets like enough, or enough rope to hang you with."

"Harry's right. Her Ladyship has run mad. No, we've taken her silver, and that will have to be our pay." A dull clunking advertised the presence of a bag full of metal objects. The departing servants had clearly looted as they left.

"Them idiots what stayed?" said a woman's voice, "if 'er Ladyship don't get 'em, and the ghosts don't get 'em, I reckon the King's soljers will."

The group had passed now, perhaps eight or nine men and women. Rats deserting the sinking ship, but Rupert was glad of it.

"Wind's getting up. We need to be across the water before the storm." The voices faded as the group hurried down the path towards the harbour.

Rupert and his companions resumed the climb until they reached the castle and hurried through the passageway into the courtyard.

"I'll leave you here," Miss Tyler said at the doorway to Lord Wyvern's tower. "Prepare Lord Wyvern to be moved. Either Shadow or I will be back as quickly as we can to fetch you."

At that moment, the door opened. "My lady!" It was Polly, Madeline's maid. What was she doing here? Rupert opened his mouth to ask, but the maid forestalled him. "I have been that worried, my lady. I thought for sure you would have gone to the dungeon where they were keeping Lord Penworth, but the guards said no one had been. But," Rupert could hear the frown in her voice, "here is my lord? Well, never mind; you are both safe."

Madeline had dropped Rupert's hand. "Polly," she said, "you must not tell Lady Wyvern we have escaped."

"Not I, my lady. Never. I haven't told about the knitting, have I? And got you as much wool as you wanted? I cut the ladder, my lady, and brought the pieces away. And I shut the window. Her Ladyship will never know how you got out."

"Well done, Polly." Madeline's voice was warm with relief.

"I serve you, my lady. Uncle is crazy to think Lady Wyvern won't be taken up for what she has done. You won't let them hang me, will you, my lady?"

"Take your maid with you, countess, and I will return to see how Shadow and Morpeth are doing," Miss Tyler said.

'Shadow' again. That was the meaning of the name Umbra, of course. Rupert was more convinced than ever that Miss Tyler and the so-called secretary served the King in that secret world Lord Wyvern had mentioned.

"Come," he said, and led the way into the tower. Madeline and Polly followed, and they were soon explaining themselves to Lord Wyvern.

Madeline and Polly helped Lord Wyvern to dress, while Rupert barred the doors at each level of the tower. He then had to unbar them again some time later, to let in the other three, their task complete.

"Now, we wait," said the man known as Shadow.

Nine

Madeline settled herself for a long wait, sitting as close to Rupert as was decent in company. The early dawn was lightening the horizon, but it could be hours before anyone noticed the Earl and Countess of Penworth were no longer in their respective prisons.

"Food," said Miss Tyler, producing a kettle and a toasting fork. She and Morpeth's supposed secretary bustled about, preparing a pot of tea and toasting bread over the fire, and soon they were sharing around butter and jars of jam and honey.

"I do not have enough plates," Miss Tyler apologised, handing those she had to Lord Wyvern and Madeline.

Polly was persuaded, with some difficulty, to sit down with the gentlefolk and have a slice of toast.

"Miss Tyler calls you Shadow," Rupert observed. "You serve the king as a…" he did not want to say spy, least the man be insulted.

The man who had been presented to Madeline as Davin Umbra grinned. "I have the honour of serving the king in this instance, my lord. He employs me from time to time when he wishes discreet enquiries to be made. And my friend here is known as Mist in my world, my lord."

"The king sent you both?"

"No," Mist replied. "As I told my lady, I was sent by your godmother, the Duchess of Haverford, when she had no reply to her last five letters."

Rupert's face lit with his smile. "She writes every month, and I dictate my reply every month. But I told the Ice Dragon Aunt Eleanor expected no reply. I hoped she would become concerned."

"Thank goodness she did," Shadow commented. "We would have found it challenging to extract ourselves from the dungeon without Mist."

"Polly," Mist said, "we saw a number of people on the path from the castle to the shore. They were leaving the island. Are many of the servants unhappy with Lady Wyvern's rule?"

"Most of them, Ma'am. Most have left already. The islanders have been coming back by night all week, taking off a party at a time."

"But you have not left," Shadow commented.

"I could not leave my lady, Sir," Polly said, moving a little closer to Madeline—whether to guard or be protected Madeline did not know. "Sam—my friend—wanted me go a week ago, but I would not go without my lady, and the rest of them said they'd not take the earl and countess till the last load, or Lady Wyvern and Lord Graviton would find out and maybe stop us. But when I went to get my lady tonight, she had gone."

"You said nothing." Rupert was not convinced, clearly. But Madeline believed Polly. "Polly, when will the boats come again? Tomorrow night?"

"Them that want to go have all gone, Ma'am. But my friend Sam said he'd wait for me till dawn."

"Will he take Lord Wyvern?" Mist asked.

Polly nodded eagerly. "And my lady and my lord. And you, Ma'am, and the other gentlemen, too. But we will have to be quick, Ma'am. The sun is coming up."

"Go and tell him to wait, Polly," Shadow told her. "We'll follow with Lord Wyvern."

Shadow contrived a conveyance by tying broom handles to a chair, so that four of them could carry it. They gently bound Lord Wyvern to it with several cravats, and covered him with a rug against the chill of the morning. Then, they carried him down the stairs and across the courtyard, Mist taking one end of a pole and Madeline hurrying ahead to check no one was about.

They made it to the harbour without any trouble and boarded the small fishing boat, where the islander crew were shocked to see their lord in such a condition. But there was no time for lengthy discussions. The rising sun was racing the approaching storm. They needed to be on the water.

Shadow and Mist, who had been talking together in low voices, announced they would be staying.

"The king will expect a report on Lady Wyvern and Sir James Graviton," Shadow said firmly.

"We must go now sirs, madams." Polly's Sam was apologetic but firm.

Madeline hovered over Lord Wyvern, wrapping the rug up higher to keep the wind-blown rain from his face, but still, she watched the two they left behind as the boat scudded swiftly away from the island dock. They didn't stay for long, soon turning to re-climb the road back to the castle.

The crew fought the wind and the sea the full half-mile between the island and the mainland, and an hour had passed before they were all safely at harbour and in a dry, warm suite in the village's one inn.

Madeline was happy to leave Lord Wyvern to the care of Polly and the innkeeper's wife, since they both seemed to know what they were doing. She came into the sitting room of the suite just in time to hear Lord Morpeth call out from where he stood by the window.

"There's another boat putting out from the island."

She and Rupert joined Lord Morpeth at the window. Squalls crossed between them and the island, obscuring the view, but then they cleared, and there was the boat, fighting its way not towards the land, but up the channel toward the open sea.

"It is a boat, Rupert, and it is in trouble. The waves are so high, and it is trying to run sideways to the wind."

Another squall crossed before them, and when it passed, the boat was nowhere to be seen. No. There it was, hull sideways to the wind, tipping and falling. They lost visibility again, and when the squalls cleared again, the boat was gone.

"The boat has sunk, Rupert. Whoever it was, they have gone down with the boat."

Rupert hugged her close and kissed the top of her head. "I feel certain it was them, Madeline. Your brother and my sister. They will never plague us again."

Rondo

Epilogue

Madeline shifted restlessly. This late in her pregnancy, she found comfort hard to come by. Rupert joked that she was carrying a couple of Old English Blacks, or possibly an elephant, but as long as he did so with his hands on her belly, his face filled with awed delight as the baby moved, he could tease as much as he wished.

Lord Wyvern murmured in his sleep. He spent much of the day in a chair by the fire, Madeline's dog, Maera, asleep at his feet. He was much improved, able to speak slowly and clearly, and to feed himself with one hand. But he tired easily.

Several hours ago, Rupert had ridden over to Clearwater Village with Simon Moreton-St Clair, Lord Wyvern's grand-nephew and heir, who was staying with them while he learned the business of his uncle's earldom.

Maera raised her head and listened for a moment. Were they coming, then? No. The dog put her head back on her paws and closed her eyes again.

"Soon, Maera. Soon."

The baby kicked vigorously, turning inside Madeline with many a push and wriggle. Soon, Baby, soon. She smiled up at the portrait of Rupert in his formal robes, painted when he was in London to obey the Writ of Summons and take up his seat in the House of Lords. Soon, she would know whether she carried the heir to the earldom, or merely his older sister. Rupert said he did not care. He was happy to help her make as many as she liked, he said, as he was rather fond of elephants.

"I loved his father, you know." Lord Wyvern was awake, watching her admire the portrait of her husband.

"He was your friend, I know," Madeline said.

"I loved him from the time we were boys together at Harrow," Lord Wyvern said. "That is why I married Louisa when she was disgraced; for Pen's sake, to spare him the shame. I did her a disservice, Madeline."

"What she did was not your fault, my lord. You cannot blame yourself for her choices."

Lord Wyvern shook his head. "Perhaps, if I had not offered, Pen could have found her a younger husband, one who shared her appetites and could have kept her satisfied. After a while—especially after Pen died—I let her go her own way."

"She chose to hate Rupert. She chose to poison you with opium and to keep us all prisoner."

"She was frightened, Madeline. When I became ill, she saw Moreton-St Clair would inherit, and she would lose all."

"Yes," said Madeline. They had discussed this before, and had worked out Lady Wyvern's motivation. An infant earl without a father would most likely be given in wardship to the mother's brother, and through Graviton, Lady Wyvern would rule the earldom. "She would not have been left destitute, my lord. She was not forced by desperation. She chose to make a grab for power."

"And died for it, in the end." Lord Wyvern shook his head sadly, but Madeline felt little sympathy. They had had the whole story from Mist two days later, once the storm blew out. Taunted with the escape of their prisoners and the imminent arrival of soldiers to arrest them, Lady Wyvern, Sir James Graviton, and their remaining servants had chosen to brave the sea rather than wait for the king's justice.

Even in death, Lady Wyvern had been a nuisance, taking over a week to wash up from the capsize, during which Lord Wyvern and Rupert had insisted on staying in the village. Graviton's body had never been found, and they had eventually left to return to Clearwater.

Maera lifted her head again, and this time uncurled and stood, then paced to the door.

"They are returned. It does my old heart good to see how you glow, Madeline. You love him, do you not?"

"I love him," Madeline confirmed, blushing.

Rupert entered and came straight to where she sat, led by the young dog, Sirius, she had been training. He leaned over to place a kiss on the cheek she presented, then turned her face with a gentle hand to kiss her on the lips.

"Rupert, you will embarrass our guest," she admonished, looking shyly at Moreton-St Clair, who had entered behind her husband.

"I am an earl, Madeline. I set the fashions; I do not follow them. And I am setting a fashion for being very much in love with my wife." Rupert kissed her again.

THE END

Please consider taking a moment to write a review of *Hand-Turned Tales*—even a sentence or two. Honest reviews help other readers to choose books they will enjoy, and help writers to gain visibility in a very cluttered book market.

News and special offers

Subscribe to my newsletter for information about publication dates and more. As a subscriber, you will receive advance information about release dates and special price periods as well as exclusive, subscriber-only special offers. I send a newsletter no more than six times a year.

You will find a subscription link at http://judeknightauthor.com

Acknowledgements

Thank you to all those who helped me put this book together: to the four prize winners who ordered the stories, to the Bluestocking Belles, especially Mari Christie and Carol Roddy, who read early drafts of some of the stories and helped me work out plot hiccups, and to my wonderful team of beta readers, whose comments and questions helped shape the final versions of the stories.

As always, a special thank you to my husband, without whose support I would probably forget to eat when I get stuck in the early nineteenth century, and to my sister Sue, who is always my first reader.

Bluestocking Belles

If you love historical romance, then you'll love the Bluestocking Belles.

We're a group of Regency romance authors providing high-quality, entertaining novels of many different styles—and heat levels—for readers who love the Regency world as much as we do.

Our blog, *The Teatime Tattler*, publishes at least twice weekly, with exclusive news, interviews, and scandals set in and around the Regency. We host a monthly book club. The Bluestocking Bookshop is a Facebook Group where writers and readers create impromptu Regency storylines as you watch.

The Belles have committed to publishing at least one box set per year. Proceeds from some of the Belles' joint projects go to the Malala Fund, to support education for young bluestockings around the world.

Find the Bluestocking Belles online:
www.BluestockingBelles.com/
Friend us on Facebook:
www.facebook.com/BellesinBlue
Follow us on Twitter:
@BellesInBlue

The Collected 2015 Editions of the Teatime Tattler

What do the Bluestocking Belles' historical romance characters do when they aren't entertaining readers in our books? Turn to the popular Regency gossip rag, the Teatime Tattler, to find out! In The Collected 2015 Editions of the Teatime Tattler, these bestselling and award-winning HistRom writers bring you a collection of short stories, interviews, cameos, backstories, and scandals, all vignettes connected, one way or another, to the novels and novellas that you know and love, illuminating our characters in ways you cannot find in any of our books.

Malala Fund

The Bluestocking Belles have chosen the Malala Fund as the charity we support, and to which we donate communal royalties. Periodically, we take on projects intended to directly support this cause, which exemplifies our personal values and intentions: the right of girls and women to do whatever they choose with their lives.

For more information about the Malala Fund and the founder, Malala Yousafzai, winner of the 2014 Nobel Peace Prize, go to www.Malala.org

Published books

Candle's Christmas Chair

When Viscount Avery comes to see the best invalid chair maker in the southwest of England he does not expect to find Minerva Bradshaw, the woman who rejected him three years earlier. Or did she? Older and wiser, he wonders if there is more to the story.

For three years, Min Bradshaw has remembered the handsome guardsman who courted her for her fortune. She didn't expect to see him in her workshop, and she certainly doesn't intend to let him fool her again. Even if he is handsomer and more charming than ever.

Farewell to Kindness: Book 1 of The Golden Redepennings

Rede believes he has turned his back on compassion and mercy. But he is distracted from the hunt for those who killed his family by his growing attraction for Anne. His feelings for her are a weakness. Or could they instead be a source of strength?

Anne protected her family from scandal and worse by changing their identity. Can she keep Rede from discovering who they are? Can she give him her heart without trusting him? Can she trust him when he has closed himself off to love?

When their enemies link forces, Rede and Anne must face the past in order to claim the future.

A Baron for Becky

Becky is the envy of the courtesans of the demi-monde - the indulged mistress of the wealthy and charismatic Marquis of Aldridge. But she dreams of a normal life; one in which her daughter can have a future that does not depend on beauty, sex, and the whims of a man.

Finding herself with child, she hesitates to tell Aldridge. Will he cast her off, send her away, or keep her and condemn another child to this uncertain shadow world?

The devil-may-care face Hugh shows to the world hides a desperate sorrow; a sorrow he tries to drown with drink and riotous living. His years at war haunt him, but even more, he doesn't want to think about the illness that robbed him of the ability to father a son. When he dies, his barony will die with him. His title will fall into abeyance, and his estate will be scooped up by the Crown.

When Aldridge surprises them both with a daring proposition, they do not expect love to be part of the bargain.

Hand-Turned Tales

Dip in, and try my writing for free: four very different tales with a variety of heroes, heroines, villains, and settings.

In *The Raven's Lady*, Felix returns home in disguise after 13 years. He plans to catch a smuggler then take up his viscountcy. He does not expect the smuggler to be Joselyn, his childhood sweetheart. (Short story: 5,500 words)

In *Kidnapped to Freedom*, Phoebe is stolen away from her plantation by a handsome masked pirate. But all is not as it seems. (Short story: 5,100 words)

All that Glisters is set in New Zealand in the 1860s, a time when gold miners poured into the fledgling settlement of Dunedin. Rose is unhappy in the household of her fanatical uncle. Thomas, a young merchant from Canada, offers a glimpse of another possible life. If she is brave enough to reach for it. (Short story: 13,000 words)

The Prisoners of Wyvern Castle is a gothic historical romance set in the world of my novels and novella. Rupert has been imprisoned by his wicked sister, and forced to wed. His new wife, Madeline, has likewise been threatened into saying her vows. Forced into marriage, they find love, but can they find freedom before it is too late? The Prisoners of Wyvern Castle is a prequel to Embracing Prudence, due for publication in 2016. (Novella: 23,500 words)

Coming in 2016

Embracing Prudence: Book 1 of *The Virtue Sisters* and Book 1 of *A Game of Mist and Shadow*

David and Prudence, operatives for one of England's shadowy spymasters, are sent to investigate a spying ring that blackmails aristocrats for access to secrets. Both find friends and family too close to the investigation for comfort.

After what happened last time they worked together, both David and Prue are determined they won't surrender to the strong physical attraction between them. They're professionals. They'll find the blackmailer and the spy behind him, and part again.

But murder, secrets from the past, and love can foil the most determined of plans

A Raging Madness: Book 2 of *The Golden Redepennings*

When Alex Redepenning comes to the funeral of Ella Melville's mother-in-law, he does not expect Ella to turn up in his bedroom, seeking help. They have met twice in the last ten years: once when she married one of Alex's fellow officers under dubious circumstances, and once when she arrived too late to attend her husband's deathbed. They parted rancorously each time.

After what he said at their last meeting Ella had hoped never to see Alex again, but an overheard clandestine conversation leaves her with nowhere else to turn.

Danger follows them; Ella's in-laws want her confined to Bedlam, and someone wants Alex dead. Joining forces is sensible. If they can survive their enemies, the only risk is to their hearts.

Lord Danwood's Dilemma: **Book 1 of** *Danwood's Daughters*

On inheriting from a distant cousin who had no sons, Anthony Simon Wentworth, the new Earl of Danwood, finds his predecessor had a unique way of stacking the odds so that a grandson of his would one day be Earl. Tony has inherited the title and the entailed land, but has no way to support it. To win the non-entailed wealth, he must marry and have a child with one of the former Lord Danwood's eight daughters.

The legitimate daughters live at Danwood Castle in the North York Moors, and in a nearby coastal village, the former Earl had a second family by his wife's sister. The eldest daughter, Sophia, keeps life on an even keel for her two sisters and two brothers, despite a lack of money and the general disapproval of the village.

Tony thinks he will settle the by-blows somewhere out of sight and marry one of the legitimate daughters. But he is distracted by the need to rescue his baseborn relatives from smugglers, the coastguard, an angry farmer or two, the machinations of their aunt—and his growing appreciation of the feisty Sophia.

Connect with Jude Knight

Jude Knight writes strong determined heroines, heroes who can appreciate a clever capable woman, villains you'll love to loathe, and all with a leavening of humour.

After a career in commercial writing, editing, and publishing, Jude Knight returned to her first love, fiction. Her novella, *Candle's Christmas Chair*, was released in December 2014, and is in the top ten on several Amazon bestseller lists in the US and UK. Her first novel *Farewell to Kindness*, was released on 1 April, and is first in a series: *The Golden Redepennings*.

Follow Jude on Twitter: @JudeKnightBooks
Friend Jude on Facebook: facebook.com/judeknightbooks
Subscribe to Jude's blog: judeknightauthor.com
Subscribe to Jude's newsletter:
judeknightauthor.com/newsletter/
Follow Jude on Goodreads: www.goodreads.com/judeknight

www.ingramcontent.com/pod-product-compliance
Lightning Source LLC
Chambersburg PA
CBHW020357130626
46549CB00006B/2312